# Billy Oliver

*Holding on to Memories*

CHARLES PETERS

Roger and Barbara Martin from Shakopee, Minnesota said *"We found this book will bring out some of the long ago memories that you had in your childhood...... We loved it. "*

Melody Vassoff from Bloomington, Minnesota said *"This is a beautiful book, full of the joys, love, sadness, and humor of childhood. As I read about Billy's experiences, I revisited many memories of my own. Read it, it will do the same for you...... I loved it, it is awesome! "*

*In memory of my biological mother,*
*an amazing woman.*

Charles Peters says, *"Some time ago, I had a vision; I sat down to the key board of my computer. At the end of the first day I reflected upon what I had just created. It was unlike anything I had ever done. I had never poured so much of my heart into a written story which was a combination of my own past experiences and fiction. That reflection gave me the desire to complete the story of Billy Oliver."*

Names, characters, places and incidents are either the product of the author's imagination or are used fictitiously. Any resemblance to actual events, or locales, or persons living or dead is entirely coincidental.

ISBN: 1461146593
ISBN-13: 9781461146599

Library of Congress Control Number: 2011907127
CreateSpace, North Charleston, SC

# Contents

# CHAPTER ONE

# Family Life

Would you like to know the Oliver family who lived in Hartlcy, Iowa, in the late 1940s? It would take an excellent memory to remember all the names because there were fifteen of us. The fourth from the last was me, Billy. With that many in the family, a meager existence was a way of life for us. I was determined to elevate mine to a higher level.

I had dreamt about this terrific place where everyone wore new clothes, had a nice big comfortable bed to sleep in, and ate ice-cold watermelon every day. I was going to run away. It was a hot Tuesday morning. I found one of Mama's cloth flour sacks, thinking it would make an excellent bag to carry some food and water. I proceeded to put three biscuits, two carrots, and a jar of water in it. That was what I was going to eat until I found this place. I left our old house behind me and headed for the railroad tracks. I had seen a few hoboes come through riding in one of the boxcars on the train. They always seemed so happy and would wave as they passed.

I thought maybe I would head away from here and join them until I found that amazing place.

When I arrived at the railroad tracks, I waited awhile for a train to come through, but there were no trains to be seen. Not knowing the schedule of when the trains were to come and go, I decided to start walking along the railroad tracks. I thought, *If a train should come along it will stop and pick me up.* I would stop only long enough to eat some of my biscuits and carrots and drink some water, and then continue on. After a considerable time, I found I had eaten all my food and drunk all my water. I was hungry and thirsty. I looked back but could not see the town anymore, and when I looked ahead I couldn't see one either. I knew I wasn't lost; I just didn't know where I was.

From the free movies I had seen downtown on Saturday afternoons about the cowboys and Indians, I remembered how the Indians would put their ear to the ground to hear if the cowboys were coming. That gave me the idea of putting my ear to the metal rail to see if I could hear anything. I listened and thought I could hear some noise. I looked up and heard *putt-putt-putt*; it was the railroad maintenance workers' trolley coming toward me, heading in the direction from which I had come. That was a welcome sight. There were two men on it. After they stopped, one said his name was Gus and the other said his name was Henry.

Gus asked me, "Are you thirsty?"

I said, "I sure would like a drink of water."

Henry got a cup of water from a big container they were carrying on the trolley. It was cold and tasted good.

Then Gus asked, "What are you doing way out here? Or are you lost?"

I spoke right up, telling them about what I had dreamt and was now looking for. Gus said he didn't know of any place like that, and Henry agreed. Then both men laughed and asked if I wanted a ride back to town. Without hesitation I accepted their offer. They let me sit near the front end. As soon as we started moving it felt like we were going really fast. The wind was blowing my hair back and felt cool. Soon we were back in town, to the shed where they kept the trolley, and that was where I got off. I walked home from there. When I saw our old house it was a welcome sight. Identifying that old farm house was not a difficult task. Looking up, there was the chimney sitting higher than the roof peak and ascending into the sky. Its opening puffed smoke from the pot-bellied stove heating the house or from the cookstove that was creating something good to eat.

Next, looking at the roof, some of the shingles were missing; it kind of looked like it was going bald. I could see the beautiful gray weathered siding. It was almost like its beard was changing color. The windows were its eyes. In the daylight, they would absorb all of nature's beauty. At night, with light from within, they would pierce the outdoor darkness.

The door was the entrance where many high-quality things were delivered. Just inside the door, the potbellied stove stood majestically in the middle of the floor. When needed, it would produce heat for the house. The bedroom in the west half of the downstairs was where Papa and Mama slept. The extra-large kitchen in the east half of the house completed the lower level.

Along the north wall of the kitchen were stairs to the second level. When using the stairs, every step made a squeaking noise. It almost sounded like someone learning to play a violin that was badly out of tune. After dark, going up or down the squeaky stairs was very scary. One of my older brothers would wait for us younger ones to get on the steps, and then he would turn the lights off, stick his head around the corner, and shout, "Boo!" The first time he did that to me, I was so frightened it caused me to pee my pants. After that, he startled me many times. I thought I would get used to it, but I never did. The single room upstairs where we boys slept held a mixture of bedroom furniture: a double bed, a couple of cots, and some mattresses on the floor. The varnished finish of the wood floor showed wear from the many feet that had walked on it.

When I was eight years old, I occasionally had to think and live like an adult. Our family consisted of four girls, nine boys, and of course, Mama and Papa. The four-room, two-level house could be very crowded at times. My oldest sister, Liz, was working and living in an apartment in Spencer, which is the county seat of Clay County, Iowa. The other two older girls, Mary and Ellen, were living with families in town. They did house-keeping chores in return for their keep because Mama didn't think it was a good idea for the girls to sleep with us boys. Five of my older brothers—Lee, Paul, Carl, John, and Steve—were away from home most of the time; either they had made a home of their own or were working and living elsewhere. Mike was about eighteen months older than me, and Tim was younger by two years. Ray went to live with the angels in heaven after ten days of life. My little sister Deb was just a baby, and she slept in a crib in Mama and Papa's bedroom downstairs.

On the south side of the house was an attached, enclosed porch. When it was new, it was a magnificent addition to the house. Now, it too was showing its age and had relaxed a smidgen, creating ventilation openings that would let in air and sunshine. It served some unique purposes, like housing the family washing machine and two rinse tubs. It also housed the wood box where fire-wood was kept dry and ready for use in the potbellied stove. It welcomed visitors who came to see our family.

Our family lived just outside the city limits. There wasn't any plumbing in the old farm house for running water or a bathroom. City sewer and water lines came to the edge of the city limits. The only time there was running water in the house was when it rained and the ceiling would leak. The landlord neglected to do any repairs on the house and failed to give credit on our rent if someone in the family made repairs. So when it was pouring rain, everyone would hurry around upstairs placing pans and pails to catch the rainwater.

There was a cookstove in the kitchen that burned wood for fuel. Each one in the family had a chore to do every day. In order to keep the wood box by the kitchen cookstove full, every night just before supper time it was my job to carry in wood to fill it. Below the kitchen was the root cellar. A trapdoor in the kitchen floor allowed entrance into the root cellar when it was cold in the wintertime. From the outside, entering the root cellar was done by opening the split doors (one opened to the left, the other to the right) that were almost parallel to the ground. The top of the doors was about a foot higher than the bottom, creating a slight downward slope from the house. This was good, because when it rained they would funnel the water away from the cellar step area.

Those doors were a wonderful place for me to lie on a warm summer afternoon. When I was lying there and watching the clouds, I thought they looked like huge marshmallows floating in the blue sky. I wondered what it would be like to walk on one of those clouds. I would then drift into daydreaming. I loved to dream, either daydreaming or during sleep. There is a difference, you know. Daydreaming is of the conscious mind and sleep dreaming is of the subconscious mind. Both ways, they were fantasies of my imagination.

I was hoping that some of what I dreamt might come true. When sleep dreaming, if I woke up before my dream was over, I wanted to hurry up and go back to sleep just so I could see what happened next. Dreams had no limits as to where I could go or what I could do. In dreams my senses of smell, sight, hearing, taste, and touch did not have the same meaning as when I was awake. When I dreamt, I let my imagination identify and build the importance of those senses.

Looking up into the sky, once in a while I would see an airplane, and I wondered how it could stay aloft. I wondered if it could see me. It seemed like it was floating, with no restrictions as to where it had to be or what time it had to be there. It looked like it was barely moving. When planes were really high in the sky, it seemed like they weren't moving at all, and I could hardly hear their engines. Some even left a white trail behind them as they moved across the sky.

I thought, *When I'm an adult, I want to fly one.* I wanted to find out what makes an airplane fly, and to look down and see how many boys were looking up at me in the sky.

Opening the root cellar doors, I could see five steps going down to another door, which opened into the root cellar. Inside the root cellar, the walls were made of stone stacked neatly in a straight line directly up and down. Cement was in between the stones to help hold them in place, and the floor was made of sand. The root cellar served a dual purpose. All the vegetables Mama canned in the summer were kept down there. It was also a great place to be in the event of a tornado. The whole family could go to the root cellar through the trapdoor in the kitchen floor and be safe until the storm blew over.

On the north side of the house we had a huge garden. As small as I was and as big as it was, standing on one side of it and trying to see the other side was an extraordinary experience. It looked like it extended forever. It was the kids' job in the summertime to eliminate the weeds in the garden. It sure wasn't my first choice for having fun. Mama always put a list of what had to be done on the entrance door so all of us could see it. That list was like saying, "Don't make any plans to be away too long," because each of us needed to pitch in with the work around home.

In the fall of the year, after Mama had completed canning the vegetables, we dug the potatoes and put them in the root cellar. Then it was time to seal the outside door. We wanted to keep all the good food that we had worked so hard preparing in the summer safe from freezing during the cold winter that was coming.

Papa worked with a man who was much smaller in stature. His name was Darrel Singer, but he was known around town as Shorty. He was a jolly man who liked to laugh a lot. He was fun to be around. Papa got to borrow Shorty's 1946 Studebaker pickup any time he needed to haul something. So he borrowed it to haul home as many cardboard boxes as we could fit in the pickup. I would help cut the corners of the boxes so they would lie flat. Then we would lay several layers of cardboard over the outside door to the root cellar. We would rake up some leaves and pile them on top of the cardboard until they were about two feet deep. To stop the leaves from blowing away, we would lay chicken wire over the top and stake it tightly to the ground. That way, the doors were well insulated and would keep everything from freezing.

All the water we used inside came from the well about fifty feet from the house. The platform that covered the top of the well was where the pump was mounted. The platform also had a trapdoor in it. We would tie a rope to the handle of a pail. We would put food in the pail and lower it down to touch the water. That way, we could keep food a couple of days without it spoiling. It was our refrigerator and seemed to work pretty well.

It became a real challenge in the winter to go out and get a pail of water. The metal pump's handle was so cold that you couldn't hold on to it with your bare hands. Papa had told us never to stick our tongue on the pump handle because it would get stuck. Being boys, we thought we might try it, to see if it was true or if Papa was just pulling our leg.

Mike and I went out to the pump when it was very cold. Mike dared me to do it.

At first I said, "No." Then I decided I would try it, but with only the tip of my tongue. So I did, barely sticking the tip of my tongue to the cold pump handle. At that moment, I knew Papa wasn't pulling our legs. I hollered for Mike to get Mama. It was like taking your fingers and pulling your tongue out of your mouth and then trying to talk. There I was, attached to the pump by only the tip of my tongue. Mama came out with a dipper full of water and poured it on the handle where my tongue was stuck, releasing it very quickly. I was no longer a captive of the pump. Mama scolded both of us and said we should have listened to Papa. "Maybe next time you will be wise enough not to do something foolish," she said. The tip of my tongue was sore for the next couple of days.

Most of the people in town had indoor toilets. There were a few that still had an outhouse. Since we lived just outside the city limits and city plumbing didn't come that far, ours was the outdoor variety. It sat right by the old barn about one hundred fifty feet from the house. Using the outhouse in bitterly cold weather was a challenge; I had to imagine I was going to war. Leaning slightly forward, I would march swiftly out to it, just like I was going to do battle. Once there I could never settle in; the seat felt like sitting on an ice cube. I would make good use of it, and moments later I would quickly surrender to the warmth of the house again.

The old barn's usefulness was minimal. Some hay was stored in the mow, and it seemed to be dry and brittle. It had been up in the mow for years. At one time enormous horses must have stayed in the barn; the horseshoe I found out there was huge. It must have belonged to one of those horses.

The town society let it be known they thought we were living rather primitively. I would like to clarify that, as I believe we were living more like pioneers.

Mama summed it up best when she said, "As primitive living goes, we are much more advanced in home life than some people recognize. We don't wash our clothes by beating them with a rock down by the stream. We don't cook our meat by hanging it on sticks over an open fire. We don't wear animal skins for clothing. People who say we live like that haven't taken the time to educate themselves. Living as pioneers the way we do is a lot of work. Good, honest work doesn't hurt anybody. It's not a lifestyle that we necessarily wanted, but it is one we can afford. Knowing everything we have is paid for and not getting something unless we pay for it is exceptionally rewarding, and it makes us incredibly proud. The fact we produce all our vegetables and some of the fruit we eat is more in harmony with the people who founded our country. We are a bit different than what they were, but they were the real pioneers. Most people who existed thirty to forty years ago had the same exact lifestyle as we have today. We just haven't converted as fast as others. In material things, we may be poor. However, our family is very wealthy when it comes to love. Each one of us has lots of it. It doesn't cost money to love. All you need to do is respect, acknowledge, be grateful, and believe in that person. This comes from the values you have been taught and from your inner you. We are living like pioneers, as most people did before converting to present-day modernization."

# CHAPTER TWO

# *Boys Will Be Boys*

Mike, Tim, and I were playing upstairs. Over beside the wall was a trunk with a metal, oval washtub next to it. The metal tub was what we used to take baths in the winter. We had to pull it over by the stovepipe that came up through the floor from the potbellied stove. The stovepipe was connected to the chimney up near the ceiling. We would carry warm water from downstairs and pour it in until it was about six inches deep. It was kind of fun taking a bath, but I had to be careful or I could burn my butt if I backed into the hot stovepipe. After all of us boys finished taking our baths, the water in the tub was far from clean; in fact, it was muddy-looking. I think if all the water had been separated from it, there would have been a pail full of dirt left.

When we opened the trunk, we had found some of Papa's old barbering equipment. Papa had quit the business years before. At that time, he used manual hair clippers, the kind you had to squeeze the handles together to make them cut hair. Electric clippers were invented by a man named Andis. He started making and selling them, and before long they had caught on all over the country. Barbers would be able to cut men's hair much quicker, with more professional-looking results. They would even take business away from barbers who still used the manual clippers. Papa decided it was time to do something else to make a living, so he took up the carpentry trade. He worked with Shorty Singer, and when the carpenter business was slow he worked with Shorty in the scrap metal business, mostly copper and brass.

We decided to play barber. Since Tim's hair was the longest, we decided he was going to get the first haircut, and then I would be next. He sat on a chair, and I wrapped a towel around his neck and over his shoulders, fastening it with a clothespin to hold it in place like barbers did downtown. Since all of Papa's equipment was operated by hand, it became quite an undertaking to squeeze the clipper handles to make them cut. I thought it would be a lot faster if I used the scissors. So with the comb I gathered up a lock of hair and snipped it. I repeated this two more times. By now I could see I had cut three nice bald spots in his beautiful head of hair.

Looking at Tim, Mike said he didn't think that had worked out so well and Tim sure looked funny. I tried to comb it different ways, but those spots showed up no matter what. Then I had an idea. If Tim were to wear a stocking cap nobody could see it until it grew out again.

With the outdoor temperature being in the eighties, Mama thought it was strange for Tim to be wearing a stocking cap. She told him to take it off. At that moment, Mike and I knew we were in trouble. For our part in the hair-cutting fiasco, she gave us a good scolding and said our punishment was for both of us to wear wool stocking caps the whole next day. Let me tell you, as hot as it was outside, it sure wasn't very comfortable wearing one. It made my head itch. I was scratching all the time. Mama said if we took them off, the penalty was we would have to wear them two additional days. With this information, I was never tempted to take mine off.

Just a couple of weeks before that, a family in town had given us a bicycle. They said it was broken. The pedals turned all the time and you couldn't coast with it. They said we could have it if we wanted it because they had already bought their son a new one. We looked at the bike, decided to take it, and thanked them for it. Mike wanted to take it apart to see what was wrong. We took it to Shorty's shop. Mike asked Shorty if he could use some of his tools to try to figure out why the coaster brake didn't work. Shorty said that would be okay, as long as we cleaned the tools and put them back in their proper place when we were done.

We turned the bike upside down on the floor of the shop. Mike began to disassemble it by taking off the chain and back wheel. He then took the sprocket assembly apart, carefully laying out the parts on a piece of cardboard on the floor. By afternoon, he had parts all over that piece of cardboard. At that point, I was sure he wouldn't ever get it back together, and we would just have to throw it in the trash.

Looking over each piece carefully, Mike found the outside space washer with tabs had worn and turned a little. That caused the whole spacer drive to jam. He said he thought he could make one if he could find a washer the same size. He looked in the box of junk nuts, bolts, and washers and found one the right size. Now all he had to do was file the outside of it to make the required tabs. He spent the next several hours filing the washer, and then shouted, "Let's give it a try!" It took him about an hour to reassemble everything, and to my surprise, he didn't have any parts left over. With the bike still sitting upside down, he turned the pedals, making the back wheel turn. He then stopped turning the pedals, and the wheel kept turning.

He said, "That is good. It is freewheeling just like it is supposed to do with no chain whip. Now is the time to take it for a ride and see if it will coast."

Sure enough, it did. The brakes worked, and we had ourselves a bike.

School was out for the summer. The carpenter business was a little slow, so Papa borrowed Shorty's Studebaker pickup truck to collect some salvage car and truck generators and starters. When he asked me to go with him, I thought it would be fun, so I decided to ride along.

Papa said, "We are going to a number of small towns today. We are going to work in a loop west, south, and then back east, working our way back home." We got started by going to the next town west, and stopped at several mechanic garages to pick up the used auto parts. The garages and mechanics gave them to us. They were happy to get rid of them. Most mechanics knew about the copper and brass, but didn't have enough or the time to do any type of salvage for themselves, so they gave them to Papa to get rid of them. By the time we got home, the pickup bed was full. We took them to Shorty's shop and unloaded them inside in a pile on the floor.

The next morning, we got up, ate some breakfast, and decided to ride our bike to Shorty's shop to see what Papa was doing. We arrived about midmorning. Going inside, we could see Papa was busy taking generators apart. He was taking the copper wiring out of them and putting it in a wooden box on the bench. He said that when he got it full, he would back Shorty's truck in and slide the box right in the truck. Mike watched Papa a while and said he had an idea that would help Papa get more done easier in the same time. He told Papa his idea of taking both ends off the generator, standing it on a ring on the arbor press, and then to use a block on top of the generator that was just a little smaller than the inside of the generator housing as a ram. Pulling the long handle of the press down would push the block through the housing, removing the copper wire in one big gob. Papa liked that idea and tried it. Sure enough, it worked. All he had to do now was cut the wire fastened to the casing and put the gob of copper wire in the box. Papa beamed with joy because he could fill the box a lot faster. Then they could take it to the metal buyer and sell it for money.

Mike looked at the pile of old generators. He pointed to one and said it was off a Ford, another one was off a Dodge, and yet another was from a Chevy. He would rattle off car names as if he knew where every one of them came from. I knew Mike was mechanically brilliant. I couldn't dispute what he was telling me; he knew more than I when it came to mechanical stuff.

We decided to leave and go home. I usually rode on the handlebars and Mike did all the peddling. That day we were going to take a different way than the way we had come. That way, we could see if there was anything interesting happening in our part of town. Going east a couple of blocks, then north, we would go right by the corner of Maple Drive and Second Street. An older couple lived there. To our surprise, when we arrived there were five men breaking up the sidewalk. I found out from one of the guys that they were going to put in a new sidewalk, starting the next day. I saw the cement mixer standing by a big pile of sand.

"We'll have to come back here and watch how they do it," I said to Mike, and he agreed.

Next morning, we came downstairs and ate breakfast. We went outside and found that the front tire on our bicycle was flat.

Mike said, "We must have run over some nails or something sharp."

We decided to walk to where they were going to put in the new sidewalk. By the time we got there, the men had already started. The old guy who owned the property came out to sit on a chair in the shade of a tree to watch them. He used a cane to walk. It seemed like his right leg was shorter than his left, which caused him to walk with a pronounced limp. He had a salt-and-pepper mustache. When he looked at you, his left eye was straight but his right eye looked off to the side. You just never knew for sure which eye he was watching with.

I went right up to him and said, "Hi, what is your name? My name is Billy Oliver."

He looked at me—at least I think he was looking at me—and said, "Hi, my name is Bert." Bert's house was the corner property of the block, so he had sidewalks on two sides that joined at the corner. He said, "You boys can watch, but you will have to stay out of the way of the workmen." He seemed nice enough from the way he told us, so I was okay with it.

We watched them mix the concrete in the mixer. One of the men would carefully count how many shovels of sand he put in the mixer. He meticulously put in the right number of shovels of dusty cement and then added the correct amount of water. He would let the mixer turn for a time period; next, he would pour the concrete into a wheelbarrow. One of the other workers would wheel it to the right place in the sidewalk forms and dump it. The other two men would push and level the concrete until the surface was smooth. The mixing, the dumping, the leveling, and the smoothing were repeated several times until the sidewalk forms were completely filled and the surface was smooth.

Bert told us not to touch the sidewalk until it had time to harden. He said, "By tomorrow at this time we probably could walk on it."

Next day, the crew of men came back and removed all the forms. They put dirt back in the proper places and even put some grass seed on it.

About a week had passed when we met up with four other boys. We all decided to play a game on Bert's new sidewalk because it was so smooth. We used some chalk and marked out a hopscotch game. We were having a lot of fun, and Bert was okay with it until he found we had also written some nasty colorful words on his sidewalk. That made him furious, and he started shouting at us. All of us boys started to run away from him. Suddenly, I stopped, turned around, and went back to where Bert was standing.

I told him, "I am sorry we wrote all those bad words on your new sidewalk. If you have a broom or brush and some soap and water, I will scrub it all off for you."

He sort of smiled and said, "I think I can find what you need, and then the two of us will scrub it off."

I thought to myself, *I think I am going to like this old guy.* He even offered to help me scrub it off.

We were about done when a nice, pleasant-looking lady came out of the house.

She asked Bert, "Who is your friend helping you?"

I was pretty sure I was going to like her because she didn't call me little.

Bert said, "His name is Billy Oliver."

She said, "Hi, Billy, my name is Grace. When you guys are done, come in the house. I have a little something for you."

When we finished and had everything put away, I followed Bert into his house. There on the kitchen table I could see a glass of milk with two cookies by it, and there was a cup of coffee with a cookie by it. Now I knew I was going to like her. Milk and cookies were one of my favorites.

"Thank you," I said. I devoured one of the cookies and drank some milk.

Then Bert said, "I want to tell you about my experience with a big fish down at the lake."

I looked at Grace and she just kind of rolled her eyes, like, *Here we go again.* Bert said he was out on the lake and it was kind of a lazy afternoon. He was dozing off, when suddenly he felt a thump on the bottom of his boat. Then he felt another, so he decided to investigate. I was listening closely to what he was telling me. He leaned over to his right and looked down, like he would when he was in the boat, to see what he could see. I was so engrossed in what he was telling me, I leaned over and looked down like he did.

He said, "I could see the eye of a fish." Then he decided to look over the other side. I did the same. He said, "I could see the other eye of that fish." Again, I leaned over and looked down like he did. Then he said, "I thought to myself, I had better reel in my line. I didn't want to catch a fish that big, because when I got it in the boat it would be so enormous and heavy it would have sunk me right out there in the middle of the lake, and I don't know how to swim. I no more than got my line reeled in when I felt the boat come up out of the water and head rapidly toward shore. There I was, the wind blowing my hair, going so fast I could hardly see. My boat was riding on the back of that big fish. When I got to shore, I was so scared. After I thought about it, I didn't go fishing for a week."

I was sitting there with my eyes really big and my mouth open. He made it sound so true I just had to believe him.

Grace said, "That is enough stories, Bert. Let Billy finish his milk and cookies, so he can go home. It is getting late."

# CHAPTER THREE

# Earning Money

There is an old saying: March comes in like a lion and goes out like a lamb. Oh, how true that was in 1948. We certainly had extremely unpleasant weather the first part of March, and then toward the end of the month the weather was very enjoyable and warm. The beautiful weather sure made me think. I asked myself, *How I can earn some money?* With the grass getting green, it gave me the idea of mowing lawns.

An older man lived just south of our house. I had seen him out in his garden or yard working about every day. He wore a long-sleeved blue work shirt with bib overalls just like mine and cotton gloves. He was an older man with thin light gray hair. He had an ever-present cap of navy-and-white-striped denim and wore it tilted sideways on his head. Talking to him, I found out his name was Zeke, and I thought he was okay. I asked him if I could call him Gramps. He said he liked that, so from that day forward I called him Gramps. His caps were cylinder-shaped and flat on the top, just like the workers wore down at the railroad yard. Seeing how nice and perky those caps were got the best of my curiosity. I wanted to know how they could look like that all the time. So one day I just had to ask him how he could make his caps look that way.

He laughed at first, and then said, "Billy, you are full of questions. I'll tell you so you will know how to make your papa's look like this. You see, when Betty washes them and they are still wct, she puts them over an empty gallon container, with the bill lying flat until they are dry. Then she takes them off the containers and brings them in the house and puts them on my shelf. The sides stay looking circular with the top being flat, which makes them nice to wear."

There was a fence between our property and his. It looked like it had been there for years; it was old and too tired to stand up straight. When Gramps was out in his yard or garden, I liked to go around the fence and talk to him. In July or August, when he would take off his gloves, his non-suntanned hands looked very pale. Mama said he dressed that way to protect from sunburn and bugs. Watching Gramps plant his garden sure gave me some ideas as to how I could help Papa plant our garden. The rows were always as straight as a string pulled tight. As the summer progressed, it was evident Gramps had spent a lot of time taking care of his garden. He kept it exceptionally clean and free from weeds.

I saw Gramps puttering around in his yard and thought it would be a good time to ask him if I could mow his lawn. I thought to myself, *I must be precise when I approach him about mowing his lawn.* I figured I would go right up to him and just blurt it out, and see what he would say. So I did.

He looked at me and said, "I think it is remarkable that you want to do something to earn money. You see, I am older with not much to do. If I hired you to cut my grass, all I would have left is working in my garden. I really want to stay busy, so I must continue mowing my own lawn." Gramps didn't have much lawn to mow, as the garden took up a big part of his yard on the north side of his house, and his detached double garage sat near the street on the south side, about three feet from the property line. "If you are serious about earning money by mowing lawns, there are a lot of other people in the neighborhood. Keep asking around, someone will want you to do it."

Just south of Gramps's place, a family had moved in about three months before. I had seen the man out in his yard; he was putting a wooden fence around it. With the fence only three feet from Gramps's garage, it looked like the space between would make a neat place for us to hide or play. The man seemed to be very busy and in a hurry. I tried to talk to him, but he always was rushing here or there. He did stop long enough to tell me he didn't want us boys cutting across his lawn anymore.

I asked him, "What is your name?"

Without hesitation, he snapped back, "Dr. Allen Redman."

I found out from the other neighbors that Dr. Redman had a wife and daughter. Dr. Redman hadn't lived there long enough for me to find out what kind of doctor he was, for humans or animals. He made it very clear for me to stay off his yard. So I knew I wouldn't be asking him. I went down the street asking the people I found home if I could earn some money by mowing their lawns. I got rejected every time. I went about three blocks south of our house and then decided to go west. I was getting the same result everywhere I went.

Then I heard some whistling and saw a man out mowing his lawn. When I got close enough to him, I could see his shirt was wet with perspiration. He had taken his hat off and started to wipe his forehead with his handkerchief. I could tell he had a twinkle in his eye, and they were a pretty blue, like mine. He appeared to be a very gentle man.

I went right up to him and said, "Hi. My name is Billy Oliver."

He looked at me and smiled. "You must be from the Oliver family that lives over there," he said, pointing in the direction of our house. "My name is Fred Hines. How can I help you?"

I told him about my idea of earning some money by mowing lawns.

He said, "Oh, that's great, because I have been looking for someone to help me with mine. I think you may be a little small, but let's give it a try."

I was so excited; I had finally found a lawn mowing job. Fred had a manual push mower. It had a cylinder-type reel that would move only when you pushed the mower. The reel would gather the grass as you pushed forward and move it over the blade, causing a shearing action between the blade and reel. He said he would mow around all the trees and his wife Bessie's flower garden, and I could mow the middle part. He told me to watch how to make the mower work, and then he went with me a couple of times across the lawn to make sure I could handle it. Watching him mow around everything, I could see the faster you pushed the mower, the higher you could get the rooster tail of cut grass coming out the back. That looked like it could be fun.

I mowed with Fred for about an hour or so when this nice-looking lady came out of the house. She was wearing an apron and had her graying hair done up in a bun on her head just like Mama. She was smiling and carrying two big glasses of what she called lemonade. She gave one to Fred and one to me.

"You guys sure look hot and thirsty." She asked Fred, "Who is your little friend?"

Fred said, "Bessie, his name is Billy Oliver, and he is going to help me this summer."

I looked at Bessie and grinned. I thanked her for the lemonade. This was the first time I had ever tasted it, so I took a sip. It was sour and sweet at the same time. I smacked my lips and thought it really was good. I continued to sip and smack my lips until it was all gone. Then we went back to mowing. It didn't take us very long before we were done with the lawn.

Fred said, "Time to do chores. Do you want to help me?"

I said, "Sure." I really liked Fred.

We went out to the barn that housed the horses. He said, "We have to get the horses in for the night and feed them some grain."

His said his horses' names were Jim and Joe. We went in the barn and opened the door, and I could see the horses out on the green grass. Fred yelled, "Jim! Joe!" and they both came running. As they got closer I could see they were huge. Their feet looked as big around as dinner plates. Fred put them in the barn and got some oats for each of them.

"You can tell them apart by the white marking on Joe's forehead." Fred started to give Joe some oats when the horse bellowed a low, loud whinny. Just then, Jim let out a muffled whinny, and Joe snorted a couple of times. Fred gave Jim some oats, and he too whinnied low and loudly. Fred looked at me and said, "Did you hear them talking to me? Joe always tells me he really likes the oats I give him and then snorts a couple of times. It's his way of saying thank you. Did you hear Jim when he made that muffled whinny? It is his way of complaining about why he can't get his oats first. Then he tells me how much he likes the oats, but he is not near as polite as Joe because he never says thank you."

A black cat emerged and rubbed against my leg. Fred said, "I think Midnight likes you. Pick him up and see if he is purring." I did, and sure enough, he was purring. I liked my new animal friend.

We came out of the barn and shut the door. Fred asked me if I wanted to go with him to his farm in the morning, if it was okay with my mom. I told him I would go home and check, but I was sure Mama would say okay. At least she would know I was staying out of trouble.

The next morning I arrived at Fred's place early. He had just harnessed the horses and had hitched them to the wagon. He was filling up four five-gallon cream cans with water. He then put them in the rubber-tired wagon the horses were hitched to.

I asked him, "What are they for?"

He said, "They are for Jim and Joe when we get out to the farm. We'll be out there all day. The horses get thirsty and need water, so we must bring some with us. Bessie has packed us a good lunch and refreshments to bring along also."

We had everything we needed packed in the wagon. Fred got up in the seat and I got right up beside him. He made a *click-click* out the side of his mouth and the horses began to move toward the road. When we got to the road, Fred said in a commanding voice, "Haw," and the horses started turning left on the road. Then he made the *click-click* sound again, and the horses stopped turning and went straight ahead. When he commanded, "Giddyap," the horses moved simultaneously into a clip-clop trot. I was amazed listening to Fred direct his horses without even having to pull on the reins to make them turn.

I asked him, "How did you teach them to do that?"

He said, "It takes a lot of time, persistence, and love for the animals. In England, the drivers of the team of horses are on the right side. When they command 'haw,' the team turns toward the driver who is turning right. When they give a 'gee' command, the horses turn left. In the United States, the driver of the team walks on the left side. The 'haw' command tells the horses to turn to the left and a 'gee' command tells them to turn right. Now it appears this could be confusing for horses from two different countries, with two ways of commanding them, but remember that Jim and Joe won't be doing any international travel for as long as they live."

With Fred whistling and occasionally singing, we soon arrived at his farm. He unhitched the horses from the wagon and hitched them to the cultivator. "I am going to get rid of the weeds in the cornfield," he said. "If you want to, pick up the rocks at the end of the field and put them in a pile over in the grove trees." Those were the rocks he found while cultivating his corn. He would carry them to the end of the field so the horses wouldn't hurt their feet on them. By now I loved the horses, so I thought I would like to do it so they wouldn't get hurt.

I started picking up some rocks, and then I had the idea of making a game out of it. First, I would draw a circle in the dirt about six feet around, stand back about five feet and toss a rock underhand into the circle. I made the rule that the rock had to stay in the circle when it landed. I would move back until I no longer could toss that far, then I would put the rocks on the pile. I counted the number of rocks I had in the circle, and that was my score. I continued this until lunchtime. Fred stopped for lunch, giving Jim and Joe a drink of water and letting them eat some grass. We sat under a big oak tree and started to eat the lunch and drink the refreshments Bessie had packed for us.

I told Fred, "The lunch and refreshments are one of my favorites." Then I mentioned, "This coming Saturday is my birthday."

He said, "Another year older, huh? Maybe we'll have to do something to celebrate. You have added a lot of rocks to the pile this morning. This afternoon maybe you should just play around."

In the afternoon, I went in the grove to mess around. I saw several squirrels running up and down and leaping from tree to tree. Listening to them chatter, I tried to imitate them. I sat for the longest time watching and practicing chattering like they did. I had a big old red one come within about ten feet of me when he heard me. I even pretended to be a squirrel; I closed my eyes and imagined I was a squirrel sitting in the nest, with the breeze making the top of the tree sway back and forth. I was beginning to get a little woozy from all the imagined movement of the tree.

Time passed quickly, and soon I heard Fred call, "Billy, let's go home." By the time I got back to the wagon, Fred had the horses hitched to it and all the other stuff picked up. On the way home I told him how I could almost make a noise like a squirrel, and I even had one come about ten feet from me. It didn't seem to be scared, but was very curious.

I asked him, "In the wintertime, how do squirrels find all the nuts they hide in the summertime?"

He said, "That is a good question, and I don't know the answer. If you come over Saturday, I will take you to the library so we can look it up. I have to go to the creamery to get some buttermilk for Bessie, so she can make some biscuits."

I arrived at Fred's house early Saturday morning. He had just completed taking care of his animals. "I'll see if Bessie wants anything besides the buttermilk," he said. She said she couldn't think of anything, so we got in the car. First we went to the library to see if we could find out about the squirrels. Fred asked the lady at the desk where we could find out about how in the wintertime squirrels could remember where they had hidden their nuts the summer before. She told us what aisle to look in and the name of the squirrel book. We found it, and Fred handed it to me to start reading. He said, "I forgot my glasses."

From the book, I learned there were three ways a squirrel knew where he hides the nuts and seeds. Squirrels rely on their very keen sense of smell first. They have been known to smell where they put their nuts and seeds in as much as twelve to eighteen inches of snow. Secondly, they use landmarks. However, landmarks can get moved, so that would cause them to miss some. The last thing they rely on is memory. Squirrels have the ability to remember about three hundred things at the same time, while humans can only remember five to ten things at once. The nice part about squirrels not finding all the nuts and seeds they hide is they will produce new plants the next year. This replenishes our trees. That is the wonderful way nature works.

Then I learned how squirrels survive in the winter when it is very cold. With their nest high in the tree, when it is cold an adult squirrel can take enough food to its nest to last seven to ten days, and it doesn't need to come out until it needs food again.

Fred thought this was interesting, and encouraged me to use the library for other things I wanted to know. That way, maybe I wouldn't ask so many questions all the time. However, I liked to ask questions and liked the way he explained things to me. We thanked the lady at the library and went over to the creamery for some buttermilk.

The creamery was located right on the main street. That made it handy for all the farmers. They would bring their cream to the creamery to sell it, and while they waited, they would go over to the café and have coffee. Once they were done having coffee, they would stop back by the creamery, collect their money and go home.

Fred always liked to get fresh buttermilk right out of the churn for Bessie to make buttermilk biscuits. He brought a cup along so we could have some from the churn. He took a cupful and drank it down, and expressed how good it was. He then filled the cup up for me. Without hesitation, I took a big gulp and discovered it tasted different from the milk I had in school. I was courageous enough to take another big gulp because Fred drank a cupful and said how good it was, so I thought I should also. Once I had a few swallows, it didn't seem too bad. We filled up the glass container Bessie had given us, paid for it, and went back to Fred's house.

Bessie asked me if I could stay for lunch. She said if I could, she had a surprise for me that afternoon. I said I could, so while she was making the buttermilk biscuits and sausage gravy, we went out to the barn to see if we could find Midnight. That wasn't hard to do because he found us immediatcly. Fied had brought some buttermilk to give to Midnight and poured it in his dish. "He sure likes it," Fred said. By the time we went back inside, Bessie had baked the biscuits and made the gravy, so we were ready to eat.

The sausage gravy and biscuits wcre good, two of my favorites. I ate so much that I thought my stomach was going to burst. Right after lunch, Bessie said, "Why don't you both go out on the porch and rest for about an hour while I finish the surprise for Billy?" I was wondering what it could be. The whole house smelled really good, like something was baking.

After a considerable amount of time had passed, Bessie called out, "It is time for the big event. Come on in and see what I have made for Billy."

As we went back in the house it smelled oh so good. There on the table was a cake, decorated with "Happy Birthday, Billy." It even had candles on it.

Bessie told me, "If you make a wish and blow out all the candles in one breath, your wish may come true." I had heard that saying before but didn't know if it was true. She then lit the candles and said, "Make a wish."

I closed my eyes and thought about it. I could wish for my own bicycle, a new Sunday school outfit, or, since Mama hadn't been feeling good, I could wish for her to feel better. I decided what I wanted to wish for, and I knew I couldn't tell anybody or it wouldn't come true. I opened my eyes and blew hard. All the candles but one went out. With a second breath, I got that to go out, too.

Bessie said, "Maybe your wish will come true." Then Fred and Bessie sang "Happy Birthday" to me. That made me feel so proud.

After we had some cake, Fred took me into their living room where Bessie had her piano. He turned the lights on and we sat on a nice cushy sofa. Bessie turned on the lamp right next to the piano, so she could see the sheets of music. I thought, *This is great. I am going to get to hear Bessie play the piano.*

Bessie pushed one key down. It was middle C. That was the indication for Fred to turn off the overhead lights. Only Bessie's lamp was providing light for her to see by. At that point, my imagination went to work. I visualized that we were in a crowded concert hall in a big city, and the place was packed. As soon as Bessie raised her hands to start playing, all those people became silent. It was so quiet you could have heard a pin drop. She played the first hymn that she would play at church on Sunday. As I watched, her fingers pressed the keys effortlessly and her hands moved gracefully up and down the keyboard, creating the most beautiful music I had ever heard. After she completed each hymn, Fred and I would stand and applaud as if we were in the concert hall. All too soon Bessie's recital was over, and I had to go home.

# CHAPTER FOUR

# *Canning Vegetables*

It seemed like every summer when the carnival came to town, it was time to start harvesting and canning the vegetables from the garden. This year was no different. The carnival arrived on a Friday afternoon and was being set up on some vacant property about a half mile from our house. Mike, Tim, and I went to watch them set up the rides, hot dog stand, and tents. Most of the workers didn't look very clean or tidy, with long hair and dirty clothes. We could see they hadn't shaved in a while. We watched them put up the tents, Ferris wheel, and merry-go-round. It all seemed kind of boring with nothing running, so we went home thinking we would come back Saturday afternoon.

Next morning we were messing around our house. I still had fifty cents in my pocket from mowing Fred's lawn. We figured there was no sense in going to the carnival because it didn't open until after lunch.

Mike said, "It would be nice to get a little more money." He had the idea of selling pop bottles.

I asked him, "Where are we going to find them?"

He said, "I'll show you if you won't tell. I have done it three times, and so far it has worked out pretty slick." He made me give my word of honor that if he told me, I wouldn't tell anybody.

I said, "I promise not to tell. I just want you to tell me."

So he began to explain how his plan worked, and that we would have to be careful so we wouldn't get caught.

He said, "I found a way that works well to get some money. We'll have to go to Willis's grocery store."

The store was located on the corner of Main Street and Maple. After we got there, he told me to follow him, so we went around the block and came in behind Willis's. Norm Willis was the owner. I had been in his store several times, and he appeared to be a nice man. It seemed like everybody liked Norm. Some of the older people would call him about what groceries they wanted, and Norm would deliver their groceries right after closing the store for the day.

Norm stored the empty pop bottles he had behind his store in a little shed. He usually left the door open during the day. When the pop truck came, he would sell them to the pop man.

Mike said he had done this three times before. We would have to be careful. We were only going to take a few so Norm would not find out. We grabbed a bottle in each hand. Mike said the best way was to walk away from the store and go past Mrs. Herman's house on the corner. I noticed she was watching us. We would go north one block, west one block, and then south one block. That would take us to the front of the store. It would look like we had found them and were bringing them in, and would be paid three cents for each of them.

Mike said, "That way, Norm won't know the difference."

Arriving at the front of the store, we walked in and said hi to Norm. He said, "How can I help you boys today?"

Mike said, "We found some more pop bottles and would like to sell them."

Norm said, "They look clean. Let me go take a look to see if I need any more pop bottles." Norm went to the back of the store and then outside.

Mike looked at me and said, "I think he has figured out where I have been getting the bottles."

Norm came back inside and said, "Mrs. Herman just called me, and I can see that four are missing."

Mike said, "Let's get out of here."

We left the four pop bottles on the counter. My heart was pounding. I was scared Norm would catch us. I ran for a ways and then looked around, back toward the store, and I could see Norm was standing out front, shaking his fist in the air in our direction. I felt bad about what I had done, but it wasn't stealing because I didn't take anything. I had intended to take the bottles, but it didn't happen.

A little later that morning I felt so guilty that I knew I had to go back to Willis's store and apologize to Norm. I went by myself. When I got there, at first I was afraid to go in, but then I remembered Mama had told me that it is best to be honest and tell the truth. With that thought, I marched right in the store and met Norm. He had his arms crossed over his chest and was looking directly at me with a cold, steely glare.

I said, "Norm, I have something I want to tell you. I am sorry for what I did this morning. I was only trying to get some more money to spend at the carnival."

Norm glared at me and I thought I was going to melt right there. I was nervous. He said, "Is that what you had in mind?" Just then, I could see his eyes soften and he began to smile. He said, "I tell you what, if you want to make some money, I would like to have you sweep the aisles in my store a couple of days a week for fifty cents a week. How does that sound?"

I said, "That would be great. When do I start?"

He said, "You can start next week, and if you do a real good job, maybe later on I will have more for you to do and will increase the fifty- cent-per-week wage."

At that point I felt a lot better. I was tickled I had another job. Then I went home so we could go to the carnival.

All we had was my fifty cents when Tim, Mike, and I went that afternoon. We found we could get three paper cones of cotton candy for a quarter. We watched some of the other kids to learn how to eat it. They would pull off a piece, tilt their head back, open their mouth, and drop it in. I thought it sure tasted sweet, and I liked it.

Then we went over to the Ferris wheel, where we could get three tickets for a quarter. The three of us got on the Ferris wheel and it started to go around. When we were at the top, I had to close my eyes because looking down scared me. When it started to move down, it felt like I had butterflies in my stomach. When we finished the ride, we could see Tim was sick. He said his head was spinning and his tummy didn't feel so good. He wanted to go home, so we took him home and told Mama what had happened.

Mike and I went back just to see what else we could see. In front of one of the tents, a man with a megaphone was yelling for all the men to come see the most beautiful lady in the world "in the natural." I sure didn't know what that meant, but a lot of men had gathered around the tent opening, paying some money to get inside.

At that moment, a large, grumpy-looking man came up behind us and unkindly said, "You boys have to move along. We don't want you here."

So we walked on to another tent. Then Mike said, "I wonder what is so secret at that tent." We decided to go back. We went around to the rear and could see the tent was loose enough for us to crawl under. We made it inside, and we could see all the men gathered around the middle part of the tent. They were hooting, hollering, and whistling. I saw the lady take the feather boa that was wrapped around her neck and fling it in the air. These grown men were acting like we kids would when we got a new bicycle for Christmas.

Each of us soon felt a large hand grab the neck of our shirts. We were marched out of the tent door and told not to come back, or we would be locked up in a big black trunk for a week. I was scared, but still a little confused. I said to Mike, "I wonder what all those men were looking at. I wonder what they were whooping and hollering about." I sure couldn't figure it out.

So without much more messing around we decided to go home.

Mama told us Mary and Ellen would be coming home the next day to help with the canning of the peas and beans. Then about mid-morning, John and Steve would be there, so we would have seven of us kids picking and washing the vegetables for Mama to can. That year Mama wanted all the help she could get because she wasn't feeling well.

Picking peas was one of my favorite things to do. I would sit down in the middle of a row and crack open some of the pea pods I had picked. Inside the pods were tasty little green peas that would burst into flavor when you put them in your mouth and bit into them.

All of us would dump the little pans we used for picking in a large pan at the same time. The first time I dumped my pan, I could see it was not nearly as full as those of the other kids. I guess I just stopped and ate too many when I should have been picking.

Soon we had the big pan full. Two of us carried it up to the house and set it under the huge shade tree. That was a nice place to put it so all of us could break open the pods and get the peas out of them. There was kind of a knack to cracking the pods open. Once I got them split, I put my thumb behind and pushed those little green round morsels of flavor, making them squirt into Mama's pan. When the pan was about half full, she would put it on the stove to cook them. It didn't take very long, and we soon had enough for Mama to do the canning process.

When it came time to harvest the green beans, Mama gave us instructions on how to pick them. She said, "Leave the stems on the plants, as it saves us having to take them off. It speeds up the canning process."

We would pick them and bring them in the house. It was like a bunch of ants gathering, carrying, and marching in single file back and forth from the house to the garden. Soon we had a huge dishpan heaped full of green beans. We always tried to put them in the dishpan laying the same direction. That way, it would be easier for Mama to grab a handful.

Mama would wash them well. She would take a meat cleaver in her left hand. With her right hand, she would grab a bunch of green beans, lay them on the chopping block, and swiftly and repeatedly chop the beans, reducing them to about an inch and a half in size. We left those little tails on the beans; Mama said that was just more for us to eat. She would then take her cleaver and scrape the chopped beans off the block into a large pan. She would always say, "Of course, the cut pieces are different sizes, but they will eat just the same." I liked to watch Mama when she chopped beans. She could reduce a huge pan full of beans into small pieces in a matter of minutes. She looked like a well-lubricated machine, starting out in slow motion until she got a rhythm going, and then speeding up. She could wash and chop the beans as fast as all of us kids could pick and bring them to her. Mama would then put the large pan of chopped beans on the stove to cook until they were almost tender. She would then stuff them into jars and continue the canning process.

After Mama finished the canning, she would set the jars filled with peas and beans out on the counter to cool. It was kind of neat to watch how the lids on the jars would indent when the hot air inside the jar cooled. That caused a vacuum, and they would make a popping sound.

Mama said, "When that happens it means they are sealed well. They have created a nice vacuum and will keep without any spoilage on the shelves in the cellar."

The next day we carefully handed the full jars down to Mama in the root cellar, and she put them in rows on the shelves. We did find a jar of peas that hadn't sealed properly. Mama said, "We will have that one with tonight's meal."

Mama canned a lot more vegetables, like tomatoes and corn—so many it is hard to name them all. It seemed like once the canning season started, Mama would be canning something nearly every day until fall. In the fall, Mama would make applesauce and apple butter from apples Shorty gave us from his trees. He said he always had more than he could use. In return, Mama gave Shorty a few jars of apple butter. Really, I think he gave Mama the apples just so he could get some of the delicious apple butter she made.

# CHAPTER FIVE

# First Train Ride

My uncle Marvin, who was married to Papa's sister, worked for the railroad and had connections to get free passenger tickets. Mama mentioned to him that it sure would be wonderful if he could get tickets for her and me to go visit her younger sister, Millie. I got extremely excited. Uncle Marvin said he thought he might be able to get tickets for us the first part of a week. He said the weekends were very busy and the passenger trains were usually full. He said we would have to leave early on Monday morning and come back home late Thursday, so it would be for only a couple of days. Aunt Millie's house was about one hundred miles to the east, near Mason City. She lived close to the train station. It would be nice to see her, because her birthday was coming up and I knew Mama had made her a new apron.

I like to go down to the train depot when the steam engine locomotives would approach and pass. It fascinated me how massive they were, with such enormous wheels. I enjoyed watching the trains being put in motion. The engineer would command the engine to move either forward or in reverse by pushing or pulling the motion lever and increasing engine acceleration with the throttle. Black smoke would be spewing out the smokestack with every chugging sound. Goose bumps would go up my back seeing the massive train being set in motion. Jake the brakeman worked for the railroad and was usually around, so I would ask him questions.

One day I asked, "When the engine is hooking up cars to pull, why is the coupling loose?"

Jake said, "It was designed that way. It makes it easy for the engineer backing up when hooking up the car and having the coupling latch. If it was made rigid the engineer would have trouble getting it to latch properly. Being loose allows the engine to move a car a little before the slack in the coupling for the next car gets tight. The engine has an easier time getting the train moving if it can start one car at a time."

I couldn't wait to be riding in one of the passenger cars while that huge steam engine pulled us along. Later in the week, the tickets arrived from Uncle Marvin. The tickets were dated for two weeks from Monday, so we had a little time to plan. I was overcome with excitement. I could feel my heart pounding. It was my dream to ride the train, and now my dream would come true. Mama said for this special occasion she would make us sandwiches with lunch meat and homemade dill pickle relish to take with us. We didn't know how long the trip would be, and that way we wouldn't get hungry.

Anticipating the trip, each day felt slower than the last. Time didn't seem to move, until finally the day arrived for us to make the trip.

Early Monday morning we went to the train station. Our train was to leave at 6:09 a.m. We got there in plenty of time because we sure didn't want to miss the train. We had to wait in the waiting room of the depot until it was time to board. As the train pulled up to the depot, we saw there already were passengers on it.

The entire luggage we had was a bag of sandwiches and a grocery sack full of clean clothes, so we got on the train and found our seats. I got to sit next to the window. It was an excellent place, where I could see everything in the country. After settling in, I heard the conductor shout, "All aboard!" This meant we would be moving soon. The ticket taker was walking up the aisle checking everyone's boarding pass. When he got to our seat, I heard him say in a nasally voice, "Folks, you are experiencing history. This will be the last week this passenger train will be pulled by that good old reliable steam engine. Next week, a new diesel engine will be pulling the train."

I was glancing out the window as the train started to move. I could see Papa so I waved good-bye. My seat was so soft and cushioned; I could hardly tell we were moving. I soon heard a clicking noise as the train started to pick up speed.

Harmonizing sounds were coming from the steel wheels under the passenger car we were riding in. When the car's wheels rolled over where the rails were coupled together, it would make a clicking sound. It was such a hypnotic and rhythmic sound that I created a little jingle. When saying it, I could remain in tempo and harmonize to the sound.

> *Big train wheels are turning,*
> *Rolling down the tracks,*
> *Taking us to Aunt Millie's,*
> *Thursday bringing us back.*

Then the clicking sound got so fast I could no longer keep in rhythm with my jingle, so I just looked out the window. I was watching a duck fly right alongside us for part of the way. It was so close it looked like I could have reached out and touched it.

I was enjoying the scenery when suddenly we came to a river. I looked out and saw that it was pretty wide, and then I looked down and quickly closed my eyes. It looked as if we were in the air because all I could see was water. I said to myself, *I hope we are not lost.* That is when I heard the train whistle tooting; we were reaching land again, entering a small town located on the riverbank. Soon we found ourselves right in the middle of it. My fears were eased and once again I felt comfortable.

Soon we were to Aunt Millie's, and we found her and her son, my cousin Randy, waiting for us at the depot. Randy was my size and age. Of course, Mama and Aunt Millie gave each other a big hug. Mama told Aunt Millie how glad she was to see her, and that she didn't know if she would ever get back to see her again. She told her that she was having some health issues and was hoping her appointment with the university hospital would come through. She said she had applied over a year ago and hadn't heard anything about it.

I looked at Randy and he looked at me. There was no way I was going to hug him out in public, in front of everyone. Boys don't do that, so we just stood there waiting to see what to do next.

Aunt Millie asked us to get in her car and said she would take us to her place. She said, "Tonight for supper we are having fried chicken, mashed potatoes, gravy, sweet corn, homemade bread with oleo margarine, and apple pie." I spoke right up and told her that sure sounded delicious, and that those were some of my favorites.

Next morning, Randy and I played out in their grove of trees. We were watching the squirrels and I told him, "I think I can make them come real close to us if we are both very quiet." I started making noises like the squirrels did. Soon we had three of them come within five or six feet of us. We watched for a while, and then Randy asked me how I learned to make squirrel noises. So I told him about going with Fred to his farm and how I made friends with the squirrels in his trees.

The morning passed so fast it was soon noon. We went in the house. They had an indoor bathroom. We had to wash our hands and face before Aunt Millie would give us lunch. She said, "That is the house rule. You have to be clean before you eat." Sure wasn't that way back home.

Right after lunch, Aunt Millie took us to a large grocery store. She needed to get some flour, sugar, coffee, and oleo margarine. I had never seen a store that big and with so much stuff in it. It was aisle after aisle of all kinds of grocery items, and in the back of the store were the meat and dairy departments.

Aunt Millie stopped by the dairy case and picked up five one-pound plastic bags of oleo margarine. It was white and soft like mashed potatoes. Aunt Millie said Randy and I could color and flavor the oleo when we got home. That afternoon, Randy and I sat on the front porch. Aunt Millie brought out the bags of oleo margarine and asked if we wanted to color and flavor it.

She said, "See this little round color-flavor pellet inside? All you have to do is squeeze until it breaks. That will let the color and flavor out. Keep squeezing the contents inside the bag to get it all mixed. It is called kneading. It is just like I do when I make bread."

This made the oleo margarine taste good and made it yellow, the color of butter. I had never done this before. I thought it was fun, but my hands got very tired from all the squeezing of the bags. She had just made bread, and while it was still warm she put some oleo margarine on it for each of us. It was the first time I had ever eaten oleo I helped color, and it sure was good.

Randy and I played hard the next couple of days. We rode his pony, Sparky. Since I had never ridden a horse before, I thought it was kind of cool. I wanted to ride it all the time. Aunt Millie had to come out and put a stop to us riding the pony. She said, "The poor thing is just a-panting and has its tongue hanging out."

I remembered what Fred had told me, that you have to take care of your horse, give it water, give it a break, and it will take care of you. So I got off and told Randy that was enough for me today; we must take care of Sparky. We could play hide and seek with some of his neighbor kids and let the pony rest. The next day we played ball and even went swimming.

Soon it was time for us to go home. Mama said she had had a wonderful visit with Aunt Millie. Then she said, "I will always remember her just like I saw her today."

The time had passed quickly and I had had a lot of fun. I was worn-out and tired, so when we got on the train to go back, I lay my head on Mama's lap and fell asleep, and stayed that way until we got home.

It was dark when we arrived. Papa, Mike, and Tim were waiting for us at the depot. Mike and Tim wanted to know all about the trip: what it was like, what we did, and what we ate. On the car ride from the depot to our house, I told them about all the things we did, all the good food we ate, and about riding Sparky. I even told them how Aunt Millie cried when Mama gave her the apron she made for her birthday.

Once we got home, I went right to bed. The next morning when I awoke, I did some reminiscing about our trip—all the fun I had had and all the food I had eaten. I decided if I ever got the chance to go again, I would.

# CHAPTER SIX

# *Flash Cards*

Summertime vacation was over, and it was the beginning of a new school year. School was dismissed for the weekend. I didn't wait for my brothers Mike or Tim; sometimes we would go home alone. I simply had to get home to tell Mama about the new game we had learned to play. I ran as fast as I could until I approached Bert's house; he was out in his garden. I was nearly out of breath, so I stopped and waved to him and yelled hi. He waved back and asked what my hurry was. He liked to have me stop and tell him what had taken place in school that day. It may have reminded him of his son when he went to school.

I was sure glad I had made friends with Bert. He liked to tell me stories, and of course I liked to sit and listen. He had my full attention until Gracie would come out and tell him to let me go home. "There will be another day for stories," she'd say. "Don't tell Billy all the stories you know in one day."

All the stories Bert would tell me were about fishing. He told me a lot of stories but never the same one twice. I had thought about some of his stories, but could never recall him going fishing, or even having a boat.

That day I told Bert I didn't have time to stop. I had something important to tell Mama, so I had to go. I started running again toward home. We lived over a mile from school. When I got there, I was out of breath. I rushed in the house and wasn't able to speak immediately.

Mama told me to calm down and tell her what was so important that I had to come rushing in the house that way.

I said, "Mama, we learned how to play a new game today, and it is a lot of fun. Mrs. Caps calls it streetcar. It is for our arithmetic class."

One of us kids would stand beside the next desk. Mrs. Caps would have us practice our multiplication by holding up what she called a flash card. The first one of us to come up with the correct answer would then stand by the next desk. Mrs. Caps would hold up another card. Each of us would try to be first to answer, to be able to move to the next desk.

The room was set up with four rows of desks, six desks in a row, which made enough room for twenty-four students. We had twenty-one students in our class. Our desks were fastened to flat pieces of wood, so they would glide across the floor easily when pushed. The room could be rearranged quickly and without much effort.

The front of each desk was the backrest for the desk in front. It had a seat that would lift up to make it easy for a student to sit down. The top of the desk was sloped downward a little, toward the student, making it easier for us to write on our papers. Right under the top of the desk was an open compartment where we could store our books, papers, pencils, and crayons.

I sat in the front row on the right-hand side of the classroom. Mike was now in my class. He sat in front in one of the middle rows. He often had his elbows firmly planted on his desk and his chin in his hands. Arthur, a kid who came from a family of privilege, sat in the front row on the left-hand side of the classroom. He always had better jeans, shirts, and shoes. He even got a zipper bag just to keep his tablet in, and he had new pencils and crayons for school. He would bring his lunch in a brand-new lunch box.

After school, he would make fun of my clothes, telling me how nice his clothes were compared to mine. I, like many others in the class, wore clothes that my mother made. A lot of the boys wore bib overalls. Why he always picked on me, I could never figure out. I was proud of the shirt Mama made for me and my bib overalls. I could put my thumbs under each side of the bib and wave my fingers like the old guys did downtown. I was so proud of my bib overalls. I even wore them to Sunday school.

For school, I would wear a homemade shirt underneath my bib overalls. On Sunday, I would put on my overalls first and then wear a homemade shirt over them. I called it my Sunday look, and would dress that way for Sunday school and special occasions.

Arthur's bragging about having things better than mine hurt me. I thought if there was any way to get back at him without hurting anyone else, I certainly would like to. I didn't want to hurt Arthur, just get even.

I told Mama the game was a lot of fun. I got to move three times before I had to sit down. Mama told me she was very happy that I was learning something new every day.

"Billy, life is about arithmetic. We use it every day in whatever we do. To begin with, let me explain about addition. When I make *fladenbrot*," she said, using the German word for fried bread, "I have already made four. Then I make two more and add them to the first four. We now have six, so the total amount is larger. Subtraction is when you take one and eat it. That makes less *fladenbrot* than we had to start. You have taken one away, or subtracted it. Multiplying is greatly increasing the total. We start with the four *fladenbrot*, and if we want to make it times two, I have to make another four *fladenbrot.* Then we have a total of eight. If we want to make it three times, I would have to make another four *fladenbrot.* Now we have a total of twelve. You see, Billy, multiplying is repeated addition. If you have four times two, which is four plus four, you have a total of eight. If you have four times three, which is four plus four plus four, you have a total of twelve. Multiplying is repeated addition, which increases the total. Division is when I take the four *fladenbrot* and cut them in half. Each one of you gets a treat, and that is dividing. We use arithmetic every day. The easy way to remember is when you add, you put more with what is there. When you subtract you take away from the amount. When you multiply, you greatly increase the amount. When you divide, you are separating into many pieces."

Mama had a way of explaining things to make it easy for me to learn. I then asked Mama if she could help me learn my multiplication table up to ten. She said, "Sure, we can get started tomorrow afternoon, after I've done a couple of loads of washing."

I got up early the next day, which was Saturday, to help Mama with the washing. We didn't have water plumbed in the house. We had to carry it from the outside pump into the house.

I took four empty pails out to the pump. I went back in the house to get the container of water we always had to save to prime the pump, so we could start pumping.

I poured the water down the top of the pump, put a pail under the spout and started pumping the long handle up and down. Soon water began to come out of the spout; I filled up all four pails, and filled the priming container with water for next time. I took it in the house and put it by the stove. Once the pump was primed, it would be okay all day and would not need to be primed until the following day.

Mama had a fire started in the cookstove. She had to heat the water in a big kettle for the washing machine. I told Mama I had all four pails full of water. They were too heavy for me to carry, so Mama carried them in the house. She poured two in the kettle on the stove to heat and two in the washing machine rinse tub on the porch. I picked up all the dirty clothes I could find and carried them to the washing machine out on the porch. Mama carried out the hot water and poured it in the washing machine tub. With a knife, she shaved off several slivers of homemade soap that Grandma gave us into the wash water. Mama put some of the dirty clothes in the machine and plugged the electric cord from its motor into the wall socket. The machine immediately started to swish the clothes one way in the soapy water and then swish them the other way, back and forth, until Mama thought they were clean.

The washing machine continued to get the clothes dirt-free while Mama took a wet, soapy cloth out to wipe the clotheslines. The clotheslines were made by Papa putting two long poles in the ground about twenty or thirty feet apart. He nailed a piece of wood across each, making it look like a large T sticking in the ground. He then stretched three heavy wires between them.

I asked Mama why she had to wipe the clothesline. She said, "I do it to clean the line so when I hang the clothes on it, they won't have a dirty streak on them from the wire."

Mama came back in the porch, and I watched her use her washing stick. Papa had made it for her by sawing off the handle of an old, worn-out broom. She used it to reach into the tub and fish out some of the clothes to see if they were dirt-free. When she saw they were clean, she would start them through the wringer, so they could fall into the rinse tub. Once she had gotten all the clothes out of the washing machine, she would take her washing stick and move the clothes around in the rinse tub to help get out any soap that might be left. She would then put the clothes through the wringer again, and this time they came out very flat. They would drop into the basket she used to take them to hang on the line. Once she got the clothes to the line, she would shake each piece of clothing to get the flatness out and kind of fluff it up a bit. Putting a small edge of the clothes over the line, she would fasten it with clothespins and leave it there to dry. On breezy days, it didn't take very long before the clothes were dry. I loved to smell freshly laundered clothes.

I then asked Mama how the washing machine worked, and how it got the clothes clean.

"Billy, you ask so many questions, but maybe I can explain it to you in a way so that you understand. When you spill water on the leg of your overalls it runs through and makes your leg wet. That is what happens when I wash them; soapy water goes right through them. Mama explained, "In the middle of the washing machine tub is what we call an agitator. It has tabs that stick out on it, which move the clothes one way and then move them the other way. The machine swishes the clothes one way, pushing them through the soapy water. There is some water going around the clothes and some water going through them. That is what loosens the dirt. The washing machine moves the clothes back the other way, pushing them through the water again and making the loosened dirt float away in the water. It continues to go back and forth until I see there is no more dirt in the clothes."

Mama always had a way of explaining things that made them easy for me to understand.

Mama completed the wash about lunchtime, so I asked, "Can you help now?"

She said, "Sure. Go out on the porch. There is a rolled-up piece of thin cardboard you brought home from Sunday school. We can write on both sides of it to make your very own flash cards."

That kind of puzzled me. How in the world was I going to learn multiplication using that rolled-up piece of the cardboard? I didn't question Mama as to why she wanted the cardboard; I went out on the porch and got it and brought it in the house. Mama then asked me to get the scissors out of her sewing basket and bring them to her. It kind of puzzled me how I would learn multiplication from rolled-up cardboard and scissors. I watched Mama as she began to cut the cardboard into square pieces.

She said, "I am dividing this piece of cardboard into smaller square pieces. We will make some flash cards just for you."

I thought, *Wow!* and beamed with joy. I felt I had the smartest mama in the world. It was nice how quickly she came up with a way to help me learn my multiplication. Now I was eager to learn more. Mama found a black crayon and began to write on the first piece of a cardboard square. She wrote a number one on the upper half, wrote another number one on the lower half, and drew a line under it. She then put an *x* beside the bottom number one and said that stood for multiplying.

I told her, "That is exactly the way Mrs. Cap's cards were."

Mama turned the card over and wrote a number one. She said, "You see, Billy, one times one equals one. The answer to this problem on the front of a cardboard square is one."

Mama took another square and wrote two on the top half and one on the bottom half, with a line under the one, and put $x$ to the left-hand side of the one. She turned it over and wrote two. She said, "Here, Billy, one times two equal two, or you may say two times one equals two. No matter which number is on the top and which is on the bottom, the answer is the same."

Mama and I spent the rest of the afternoon making my very own flash cards. In the late afternoon, when we had completed my flash cards, Mama said I should look at each one and memorize them while she made supper. I was so excited about my new flash cards; I didn't even mind her telling me that we were having hamburger gravy, mashed potatoes, creamed carrots, and homemade bread again. It was one of my favorite meals. Sometimes she would add some breaded tomatoes, which always tasted good.

After supper, I wanted to play with my new flash cards, so I put them in a pile on the floor with the answers facedown so I couldn't see them. I would close my eyes and reach into the pile to get one. I would pretend I was Mrs. Caps and hold it up. When I opened my eyes, I would have to know the answer.

At first, I had to take some time for each card. The more I played with the cards, the faster I would get the answer.

Late Sunday afternoon, Mama said, "I want to see if you have learned anything." She would hold up the cards, and I would shout the answer. Mama was very pleased with how quickly I answered and got every one right. I could hardly wait for Monday to come so I could get to school.

Mrs. Caps had said we would play streetcar again on Monday. So when I got to school I could hardly wait for arithmetic class.

Finally, the time had come. I got to be first, so I stood up beside Sally's desk. Mrs. Caps held up a card with two times three. I was quick to answer six. That was right, so I got to move to the next desk, which was Jordan's. Mrs. Caps held up a card with four times five. I was quick to reply twenty, so I got to move again. This was done over and over, the way the game was played, and at each student's desk I stood by I was first to get the answer. I made it clear around the room, up to the last desk, that being Arthur's.

I stepped forward to stand beside Arthur's desk and thought, *Now is my chance to get even.* I could do this in front of everyone in the class, and would surely get back at Arthur for the things he had been saying about me.

Just then, I was disappointed. I could feel the hurt inside and had a lump in my throat. I had to hold back the tears. The school recess bell had rung. I would never get to compete with Arthur. Class was over and all the kids were hurrying outside to play.

# CHAPTER SEVEN

# Mama's Appointment

A couple of days after school had started again, Mama received what looked like a very important letter in the mail. It was from the university hospital. Mama read it and had tears running down her face. She said, "Billy, I finally have my appointment. I have to be there next week." She asked me to go over and tell her mother, Grandma Planter, who lived on the other side of town.

I always thought it was kind of creepy going to Grandma Planter's because she lived alone in a smaller-than-average house that she kept dark inside all the time. She only had one wire that came down from the ceiling, with a small bulb screwed into its socket. There was a string hanging from it, which was used to turn it on and off. It didn't illuminate the area very well.

In the past, Mama would walk over to see Grandma about once a week and visit with her. Now that she was not feeling well, she didn't think she could do it any longer. Since Mama asked me to go tell Grandma the news about her appointment, I told her I would do that for her. I was willing to do anything for my mama.

When I arrived at Grandma Planter's, I could see the house was dark inside. She lived in a self-imposed exile, with very little contact with people. I think she had to live that way because she didn't have much money; she depended upon charity and welfare. Despite her meager existence, she always appeared to be joyful and happy.

When I knocked, it took her a little while to get to the door. It was thought that she might have had polio when she was younger and lived in Germany, and now she couldn't walk without some sort of aid. She used a wooden chair in the house. She pushed it around holding on to the back of it. That worked well. She had used it so much the legs on it were worn down to the first rung on the chair.

She always had her hair done up in a bun on top of her head. She had false teeth that were way too loose. When she would talk, her false teeth would make a clattering sound. Whenever she spoke German, I didn't understand what she was trying to tell me. Grandma could speak some broken English. When she tried to speak English with her teeth clattering at the same time, I just couldn't comprehend what she was saying. If she got very excited, she would mix German and English together simultaneously. Then I was really lost.

I told her that Mama's appointment had come through, and she had to go to the university hospital next week. Mama didn't know how long she would be gone. They were going to examine the lump under her left arm and see what they could do to relieve some of the pain. Mama said she was having my two older sisters who lived in town come home and stay with us boys. They would be using her bedroom while they were there.

Listening to Grandma, I made out a little of what she was trying to tell me. I thought she said she was glad for Mama's appointment and would be thinking about her. After that, everything she said with her teeth clattering was unintelligible.

I came home to tell Mama that Grandma would be thinking of her and hoping she would have a safe trip.

I went outside to play for a while, and then my older brother Steve came home. Steve had dropped out of school and was going into the army in a couple of weeks. He was too young to get in by himself, so Papa had to sign for him to get him in. He was home to spend some time with us younger boys before he had to report for duty.

For something to do, he asked me if I wanted to go hunting with him. I thought that might be fun. He had an old car that didn't run very well, but he said it would get him where he wanted to go until he had to go to the army.

He drove us about a half mile south of town and stopped by a grove of trees. He said, "Look! There are a couple of squirrels in the trees."

I said, "If you look at squirrels, they are so ugly that you just have to love them."

I got out of his car to get a closer look. Suddenly, I heard *bang*—then *bang* again. I watched those two squirrels fall from the tree. I went over to them and found that they were dead. I didn't know he was going to shoot them. He picked them up and put them in his car. He then asked me where Fred's farm was, because I had talked about all the squirrels that were in his grove of trees.

I looked at him in disbelief. I said, "You killed them. Squirrels are my friends, and I am not going to tell you anything. As a matter of fact, I don't even want to be with you. You want to know where my friend's squirrels are so you can kill them, too. I'll just walk back home. I don't want to be around you."

I started to walk home. He turned his car around and drove up beside me. He asked me to get in, and said he would take me back home. I told him I wouldn't ride in a car with dead squirrels, especially since he shot them.

When I got home Steve had already told Mama what had happened. Mama explained to me that Steve didn't know I liked the squirrels so much. She said he was hunting for game, just like he had every year. She said actually it was not a very popular source of meat, but she had fixed it before and squirrel could taste great if cooked correctly. She said Steve felt bad. He didn't know I liked the squirrels so much, and he said he wouldn't hunt around there anymore.

That made me feel somewhat better. I thought, *If Mama cooks those two squirrels, I know for a fact I won't be eating any of them. I'll go hungry first.*

Mama's health had been declining, and I was sure glad she could get her appointment. I knew she would be gone for a few days, but there would never be a day that went by without me thinking of her. Mama made arrangements for Mary and Ellen to come home to stay with us boys. They were both in high school and it always got out early, so they were home before us.

The next morning Mama left for her appointment. Papa said it would take two days to get there. He told us boys to do what Mary and Ellen asked us to do. He said, "Mary is a pretty good cook, so you won't starve to death before we get back." I gave Mama a big hug, and told her I would be thinking of her and to have a safe trip.

The very first day Mama and Papa were gone, Mary had something to do at school right after class, so she stayed a couple of hours to take care of the project she had been assigned. Ellen had already come home from school and was going to show us that she could cook, too. She was a little strong willed and most of the time wanted to do things her way.

Right away, she said, "I am going to bake some bread. I have watched Mama enough times that I know by now how to do it."

I watched her carefully measure the flour, shortening, and water. She mixed it together and divided it in the four greased bread pans. It looked pretty flat to me, but Ellen said, "It will take a few minutes to rise. I am going to take a shortcut and start baking the bread. The bread will rise quicker in the warm oven."

When the bread was about ready to come out of the oven, I asked Ellen, "Did you remember to put in the Red Star yeast?"

Suddenly, her face drained of all expression. She said, "I knew I must have forgotten something because the bread looked so flat when I put it in the oven."

She opened the oven and retrieved the four bread pans, and said it was a little darker brown than she wanted it to get. To me, it looked as flat as when she had put it in the oven. For her to say it was brown wasn't quite accurate—it was almost black. She let the bread cool and told us it might not look like the best, but it would be satisfying.

Once the bread was cool, Ellen tried to cut it with a knife, without success. She then placed one of those flat loaves on the chopping block and used the meat cleaver to whack off a piece. She wanted me to try eating it first. I thought to myself, *Oh, how I wish Mama was here.* I was not sure if I could even bite into the piece of bread Ellen gave me. I was afraid if I accidentally dropped it on my plate, it might break the plate.

When Mary came home and saw the disaster, she said, "All is not lost. We can feed it to the birds."

I took some outside for the birds and watched. Some of them tried to peck a crumb from it, but would give up and fly away.

Mary said she had some money in a savings account, and if we had to use it before Mama got back home it would be okay. She had some money in her pocket from babysitting last week, so she gave it to me to go to the store to get some bread for supper and for our lunches tomorrow. Mary was nice and understanding. She helped us all she could and still maintained her B average in school.

About ten days passed. When I came home from school, I saw Papa's car in the driveway. I got my hopes up that Mama would be in the house, too. When I went in, at first I didn't see her because she was resting in bed. I went up to her, wanting to give her a big hug because I was so glad to see her. However, I stopped. She looked different.

I proceeded very cautiously and asked her, "What happened? You are flat on one side of your chest."

Mama said, "The doctors at the hospital told me I am very seriously ill. They told me that my best chance to live longer was to have surgery, and they would try to remove all the cancer. They removed my left breast because it was full of cancer. The doctors did the best they could, and I am hopeful they got all of it."

Then she showed me the incisions they had to make. I was kind of squeamish and felt woozy at that point.

I told Mama I loved her and wanted to give her a hug. She said, "Come around to my right, but be very careful. I want to give you a hug, too."

Mary and Ellen stayed with us a while longer, until Mama got some of her strength back. With a little coaching from Mama, Ellen even learned how to make some pretty good bread.

I liked going to school. We had an interesting teacher who made it fun to be there. Right after school I always went by Bert's house. He'd be outside, like he was waiting for me. I loved to sit and listen to his fish stories. How many were true, if any, I'll never know. He always got my full attention. He could get me so interested I even made some of the same motions he did when he was telling them. I could listen to his stories by the hour. I don't think he told the same one twice, not that I can remember.

That day I wanted to tell Bert that in a couple of days I was going to my grandma's for Thanksgiving dinner.

He asked me, "What are you going to have, turkey?"

I said, "No, Grandma makes the same thing every year, and its noodles, chicken, and dumplings. It is one of my favorite meals."

A couple days passed, and soon it was Thanksgiving and time for us to go to Grandma Oliver's to eat. Grandma was Papa's mother. She had to make the noodles a couple of days before Thanksgiving. She would hang them over the back of kitchen chairs so they could dry. They were always big, thick, flavorful, and tender. She would cook them, as she would say, "with a couple of fat hens," along with dumplings that only she knew how to make. All I know is it all tasted delicious, every time.

When we got to Grandma's house, I told her how glad I was to see her. I said, "If we ever had any more kids, there would be so many that we would have to come in a bus."

That year she said she had something different. She said, "It is a surprise, and you will have to wait until dinner to find out." When she called us for dinner, I could see a big bowl with dark red stuff in it. I asked her what it was, and she said, "That is my surprise. It is cranberries."

I told her I had never eaten cranberries. I looked at the noodles, chicken, and dumplings and told her that those were my favorites, but I didn't know about the cranberries.

She said, "I am sure you will like them," and then watched with great joy as each of us kids tried a bite of cranberries. We each had a first reaction of puckering up. Those cranberries were tart and sweet at the same time. After trying them repeatedly, I began to like them.

I had eaten so much I thought I was going to burst. Then Grandma brought to the table a delicious-looking pumpkin pie. I told her I had eaten so much I didn't think I had room for pie.

She said, "We will wait until the middle of the afternoon, then you can have some just before you go home."

Soon it was time to go. Mama was feeling a little weak and she wanted to lie down at home.

Grandma said, "I will just have to send some goodies with you." She put some noodles, chicken, and dumplings in one of her pans. She handed it to Papa and told him he could bring it back when it was empty. She also sent along a nice pumpkin pie. I knew that wouldn't last long once we got home.

When we got home, Papa cut the pie in smaller pieces so each of us kids would get some. I took mine into the bedroom where Mama was resting. I wanted to share it with her. For the next few minutes, she and I enjoyed that piece of pumpkin pie.

# CHAPTER EIGHT

# Enjoying Winter

On Sunday evening, we had our Christmas program at church. We had been practicing for a couple of weeks. I did all right in practice, but now we were going to perform in front of a whole church full of people. We did basically the same thing every year, and every year I had just as many butterflies. We had Mary and Joseph, with a doll as Jesus in a cradle in the manger, wise men, and shepherds. If we had a lot of Sunday school kids appear for the program, we had a lot of shepherds. I was one of the shepherds. We got to wear white sheets over our shoulders that hung to the ground, and we carried a long stick like we were herding sheep. I am not sure if that is the way sheep were herded, but that is what the Sunday school teacher told us.

Then, right after the program, we all got a sack of treats, with an apple, an orange, a popcorn ball, and some hard candy in it. I would wait until I got home to open my treat sack, and then I liked to share it with Mike and Tim. I would divide the apple into six pieces and slice the orange in six pieces so each of us would get two. Then I gave two pieces of hard candy to each of us and sometimes had an extra one left, which I kept for myself. The year before Mike got the popcorn ball, so this year it was Tim's turn. I was the only one who ever went to Sunday school.

Mike said, "I have had enough school."

Tim said, "I don't like it."

Even though we didn't have a Christmas tree, we had presents to open on Christmas Day. That year I got some new overalls and underwear. I was glad to get the underwear because the ones I had were full of holes. I said, "This is my Sunday underwear because it is holey."

In a big box, I got a thousand-piece jigsaw puzzle. The picture on the box was of a horse. That would keep me busy for a while. I put all the pieces on a large piece of cardboard, turning them faceup. That way, it would be easier for me to fit the pieces together. When I had to stop, I could carefully slide it under my bed. The next time I wanted to continue, I could slide out the cardboard, and it would be right there on the floor, handy for me.

The Christmas holidays were soon over and we had to go back to school. It was cold. We were getting one of those wintry blasts we got several times each winter. It wasn't very comfortable to be outside. The teacher told those of us who had to walk a distance to get home to be sure not to stay out in the cold for more than fifteen minutes at a time. She said, "Try to find someplace where you can get out of the cold every once in a while." Then she asked, "Does anyone need help getting home?"

I didn't think I did, but when I was coming home from school, walking all huddled up trying to stay warm, I wished I would have asked for some help. It was brutally cold. My nose and ears were freezing. With every breath there was a cloud of vapor. I knew that was the moist air coming out of my mouth and immediately freezing in the cold air. I was doing my best to stay warm. I was walking backward into the wind, making progress toward home, when unexpectedly I heard a car stop alongside the road and toot its horn. I looked up and, recognizing that shiny blue 1939 Buick, I knew it was Fred and Bessie Hines.

Bessie rolled down her window and said, "Billy, get in our car. It is too cold out there for man or beast."

After I got in the backseat where it felt warm, Fred said, "Billy, how would you like a belated Christmas present?"

I thought a little before saying, "Sure, that sounds great. I am always happy to get a present."

Fred turned his car around and drove back downtown. We parked in front of the clothing store. Fred said, "Let's go in and see if they have anything that will fit you." Then he looked at me and winked.

When we got inside the store, we went over to the coat section for boys. Fred said to the clerk, "I want to see if you can find a nice warm coat for Billy." To me, he said, "Look around, Billy. Find the one you like."

So I looked and looked, and even tried on several. There were so many to choose from, but I finally found the coat I liked. It was dark brown in color, with a collar I could turn up to help protect my ears, and it had six buttons down the front.

Fred said, "Billy, you have made an excellent choice. It is reasonably priced and it looks like it will keep the wintry temperature out." He then told the clerk to find me a warm cap, mittens, and overshoes. The clerk checked my shoe size and went in the back room to retrieve the correct size overshoes. He picked up mittens and a cap off the shelf and took all the items up front to the cash register. He figured what the bill would be, and Fred gave him the money for it.

I put on my new coat, cap, mittens, and overshoes. I took the bag the clerk put my old coat in and put it in the backseat of Fred's car with me to take home. I sat right in the middle on the edge in the backseat. I was as proud as a peacock. For the first time in my life, I felt like I was somebody. Fred backed out of the parking space and started down the street. I told Fred, "Don't drive too fast. Let's take it real slow." I wanted everybody to see me now. I felt like an important person. I looked to both the left and the right to see if anybody was looking, just so they could see how significant and important I looked. I was so proud of my new coat. I thanked Fred and Bessie a couple of times for buying it for me. I even managed to give Bessie a big hug.

Fred said, "Billy, this is a belated Christmas present. We love to have you come to our house and help out. We like it when you play with Midnight because at times he seems to be so lonely. We like you helping with other chores."

Fred drove slowly, just as I had asked, and he even took me home. He wanted to talk to Mama, so I went in the house and told Mama that Fred was at the door.

Fred said to Mama, "I hope you don't mind, Mrs. Oliver, but today we bought Billy a new winter coat, as a belated Christmas present. He helps me a lot when he comes over and we sure enjoy having him."

Mama said, "I understand. Thank you, Fred, this is a nice gesture."

When Papa came home that night, I showed him my new coat, mittens, cap, and overshoes.

He said, "They sure look like they'll be warm. Do you want to try them out this weekend? We could go do some ice fishing." I think Papa went fishing every chance he could. He was almost addicted to it. He said, "You will want a warm coat because it is so cold out on the lake."

I thought that sounded like fun, and it was something I had never done before.

Sunday came and we loaded up the car with our fishing equipment, made some lunch to take with us, and headed to the lake.

I asked Papa, "What are we going to use for bait?"

He said, "I will show you, as soon as we get closer to the lake." Soon we were close enough, so he said, "We have to start looking for bait. Corn borers will make good bait for perch."

I said, "Where do we look for them?"

He said, "In the cornfields."

I asked him, "Where do they come from, and how do they get there?"

He said, "The whole cycle of a corn borer starts out in the summertime. As a moth, it lays its eggs on the corn plant. When the eggs hatch, the larvae, which looks like a worm, burrows its way into the cornstalk and feeds off the plant, making it stronger so it will develop into a moth. But this makes the plant weaker and it won't stand up straight, and sometimes makes the cornstalk fall over. When it gets cold and freezes, the larvae that haven't hatched will hibernate in the stalk close to the ground. That is what we will look for today. Perch love the larvae. See that cornfield to your right? That probably won't have any borers in it because the stalks are still standing pretty upright. Look over here, up the road on the left side. See how the stalks are more bent over than the last field?"

He stopped the car on the shoulder of the road and went out in the field. He showed me how to cut off a stalk and split it open to look for borers. Right away he found one and said, "This will be good bait for perch." We continued to look and found about a dozen more. Papa said, "It is time to go fishing."

We drove up to the lake and turned right out on it. For a moment, I thought we were going to go right through the ice.

Papa said, "I would never drive on the ice if it was only about a foot thick."

When we got out of the car and cut a hole in the ice to put our lines in, I found the ice to be about twenty-two inches thick. That was plenty thick enough to hold us. It still made me very nervous when cars would drive close by and I could hear the ice pop and crack. In about an hour that afternoon we caught seven perch.

Then Papa said, "We have to get off the ice before dark." He didn't like being out there in the dark.

We packed up our fishing lines, put the fish we had caught in an empty pail, and headed for home. I stayed warm all afternoon. I was glad Fred and Bessie had bought me the new coat.

When we got home, Papa cleaned the fish on the porch and got rid of the waste outside. He had fourteen nice pieces of fish, and if Mama was feeling good enough she would fry them for supper the next night.

Valentine's Day was coming and I had a crush on a girl in my class. She had light brown hair. She liked to wink and smile at me a lot. Of course, I liked that. Her name was Joy Reed. I told her, "I think Joy is such a pretty name." For Valentine's Day, I drew a heart on a piece of paper with an arrow through it. Underneath, I wrote "Be Mine," and gave it to her.

I didn't wait for Mike or Tim after school because I wanted to carry Joy's books for her. She lived a little out of the way of my house, but I was thrilled to do it.

Right after Valentine's Day, her mother found out who I was and where I lived. I had walked Joy home, carrying her books for her, when her mother met us at the front door.

She said, "I don't want you to be around Joy anymore. I know your name is Billy Oliver. I want Joy to be associated with better friends than the trashy, poor person you are." Then she grabbed Joy, pulled her in the house, and slammed the door.

I was shocked at what had happened. I couldn't believe how just a few words could cut me like a knife. I went home and told Mama about it, and how it made me feel so bad.

Mama said, "Billy, you have just had your ego bruised. They are only words and you must consider the source.

Nobody has ever given her authority to judge other people. There are people like Mrs. Reed who judge by the material things they see and where people live. Those types of people have shallow values. They are not able to handle life's daily challenges that come along without a lot of stress and constant worry. They judge people for what they think they are.

There are others who will judge people for who they are. They will respect the knowledge you have, the love you exhibit, the understanding you express. Their values run deep, and they are able to handle the daily challenges with ease. Knowledge, love, and understanding are some very good traits to have, and they will help you build a strong set of values that you will use throughout your life. Knowledge is something no one can ever take away from you. Like when you are carrying a book and someone comes along and takes it. You have lost it. If you had read the book and learned what is in it, then if someone takes it, you still have the knowledge. Love is what you exhibit. It's the caring for people, places, and things. Understanding is showing how you care.

"I want to tell you a story I heard when I was a growing up. It's about a young boy living in poverty in a log cabin many years before me. The family didn't have many material things, so he had to read his books by the light of the fireplace. I am sure he had heard many times how he was a trashy, poor person coming from such a meager home setting. He had the intestinal fortitude to read as many books and learn as much as he could while growing up. He became a very respectable citizen whom everyone looked up to and admired. He was one of the greatest men of his era, and he became our sixteenth president. His name was Abraham Lincoln."

# CHAPTER NINE

# *Doing Right*

When I came home from school one spring day, I saw several lawns getting really green. It wouldn't be long before I would be able to mow Fred's lawn again. That gave me the idea of going over to Fred's to check when he wanted to do it.

When I got there, Bessie was surprised to see me. She said, "You have grown since last winter, when it was so cold. Fred is out at the farm, but should be home all day Saturday."

I told her I would come back Saturday to see if Fred had anything for me to do, and to see when he wanted me to start mowing.

I went to Fred's early Saturday morning. I found he had his beloved horses Jim and Joe hitched to a plow and was plowing Bessie's flower garden. I watched him. I was amazed how well his horses responded when he would give them a command. When they had pulled the plow to the end, Fred would command "gee" and immediately they would turn right. When it was time to put the plow back in the ground, he would make the *click-click* out the side of his mouth and the horses would go straight. Once the plow was in the ground I could see the team pull as hard as they could. I think they really liked to be challenged by the work of pulling the plow. I sat in the shade and watched Fred give commands, repeating the process of plowing. Soon he had the entire garden plowed.

Fred stopped long enough to tell me he was glad to see me. He said, "I will put the horses away. Would you help me pick up sticks in the yard?" It didn't take very long, and we soon had a pretty good-sized pile. "I am going to burn them," he said, and then looked at me. "I have an idea. Billy, how would you like to have a wiener roast? And maybe afterward we could even roast some marshmallows."

I had never roasted wieners or marshmallows, but it sure sounded like fun to me. I told Fred, "That would be exciting."

He said, "We'll ask Bessie if it is okay with her, and then we need to go to the store. We need to get some buns, wieners, and marshmallows."

Bessie thought it was a good idea. She would make some refreshments. She said, "It would be fun."

So off to the store we went. When we got back from the store, Fred showed me how to cut a nice long stick from a live tree and sharpen one end. He said, "You should use a stick that is green so it won't burn when we hold it over the fire." We poked the sharp end of the stick into the end of the wiener. Fred said, "We'll have to turn them frequently so they won't burn. When the wieners are done, we'll put them in a bun, hold them while we pull the stick out, put some mustard on our hot dogs, and they will be ready to eat."

After I had done two wieners, I ate them and thought they were really tasty. They quickly became one of my favorite foods.

Once finished with the wieners, we started roasting the marshmallows. We had to be careful because they burned so easily. We put some on the sticks and constantly turned them. We got some that turned out a nice golden brown color and were scrumptious.

I thanked Fred and Bessie for inviting me to their wiener roast. I told them, "It was fun, but I think it is time for me to go home."

Fred said, "I understand. I want you to come back next Saturday to mow my lawn. It should be ready by then."

Sunday went by in a hurry. When we got up Monday morning, we knew we didn't have school because of spring break. The weather was getting warmer, and we were always looking for something to do.

We had to walk past Dr. Redman's house on the corner several times a day. I had watched him erect a fence around his yard the previous year.

He had said, "It is to keep you boys away from my house. I don't want you to cut across my yard anymore, and you are to stay off my property."

I did find out he was a veterinarian. He was always busy taking care of animals.

Walking by his property on the dirt path between his fence and the street, I could see that his little daughter had been playing in the sandbox with her piggy bank.

I said to Mike, "I would like to see what is in her piggy bank."

He asked, "How are you going to get it and not go on Dr. Redman's property?"

I said I would use a stick and a string. First, I looped the string over the end of a stick, and then I sat on the outside of the fence in our little hideaway hut between Gramps's garage and the fence. There was a big knot-hole in Dr. Redman's fence right there.

I told Mike I thought I could fish the stick and string through the knothole toward the piggy bank. I thought I could get the string over the head of the piggy bank.

Sure enough, I did, and at that point pulled the string tight and drew the piggy bank toward the fence.

When we got it beside the fence, Mike said, "The only way we can get it now is to dig under the fence and grab it."

We dug an opening right where the bank would be, and I reached under and grabbed it. It sounded like there was some money in it from the way it rattled. Mike took the bank and got the bottom open, and sure enough, there was money inside. The money fell out when Mike opened the stopper. So he put some rocks in it and replaced the stopper.

He told me to put it back in the sandbox and nobody would know the difference. Dr. Redman would just think that Lisa had lost her money when she was playing with it outside.

I asked Mike, "Isn't this stealing?"

Mike said, "Stealing? I am not stealing anything. I found that money on the ground. You know about 'finders keepers, losers weepers.'"

The next day at noon, as we were walking by, Dr. Redman stopped us. He said that Lisa had told him that she had seen us by the fence. Right after we left, she had checked her bank, and it didn't sound like it had coins inside. She told him that she opened it and found rocks inside, and that the Oliver boys must have taken her money. He asked, "Why did you boys take her money?"

Mike and I said we didn't know what he was talking about and that she must have lost it.

That didn't sit well with Dr. Redman, and he firmly stated, "I don't want you boys on my property at all. I am sure you took her money, and that makes you thieves."

I felt guilty and couldn't even look him in the eye. I knew we had to stick to our story because we had already spent the money. Mike and I left in a hurry, and we ran all the way home. When we got home, we went out in the old barn.

I told Mike, "It sure bothers me about that money. If it looks like I am guilty, it is because I am."

Mike said, "He didn't prove anything. Besides, I found the money on the ground outside the fence."

For the next few weeks, I thought about that money, and I knew we had done wrong.

On Saturdays, I would go over to Fred's and mow his lawn. When Bessie wanted to pay me a dollar, I told her to save it for me because I had a plan.

After three Saturdays, the money she had saved for me totaled three dollars. After I was done mowing, I asked, "Can you pay me? I can't stay for the refreshments. I have something really important to do." She paid me, and immediately I started in the direction of home.

I went to Dr. Redman's house. I almost chickened out, but I got up the courage to knock. Mrs. Redman came to the door.

I asked, "Is Dr. Redman home?"

She said, "No, and you know you aren't supposed to be on our property."

I said, "I really need to talk to Dr. Redman. Would it be okay if I sat on the steps and waited for him?"

She said, "Do as you like, but you know he is going to be upset when he sees you there."

I sat on their front step. I was very nervous. When I raised my heel off the step, my leg would get to jumping up and down uncontrollably. All the while, I was thinking to myself just how surprised he would be to see me give the money back and tell the truth. I felt he would tell me how nice it was to know such a remarkable young boy. I thought he would tell me how proud he was of me. I just knew he was going to make me feel first-class.

About twenty minutes later, Dr. Redman came home. The first thing he said to me, in a grumpy voice, was, "What are you doing on my property?"

I said, "I have something to tell you. Remember about three weeks ago you thought we had taken Lisa's money? All I can tell you, Dr. Redman, is that we took the money, and here is three dollars to repay what we took."

He took the money from me, then he shook his finger at me and said in a thunderous voice, "I knew you two were a couple of thieves. I have told you before to stay off my property. Now I am telling you to get off it and never come back." He went in his house and slammed the door behind him.

I was scared. I immediately ran out to the road just so I wouldn't be on his property. I had never expected such an outburst.

I started to run home. There was a powerful amount of emotion twisting around in me. I was kind of confused, feeling both cheerful and miserable at the same time. I was very happy that I had done the right thing. I could hardly control myself, I was so proud. At the same time, I was heavy-hearted from the way he had told me to stay off his property. I was disappointed. I felt about as low as a person can get. I was so filled with emotion that tears were running down my cheeks uncontrollably. I was at a loss. I had been so sure that I was doing the right thing.

I came running in the house nearly out of breath. I had to make it clear to Mama what had happened. She was so dear about it. She sat and listened, putting her arm around me. After I had told her the whole story of what had happened, she said, "Billy, you have just learned an important lesson about life. You must make it right and forgive yourself of wrongdoing before you can ask forgiveness from anyone else."

I said, "I tried to make it right. I did with myself, but not with Dr. Redman."

Mama said, "Oh, yes, you did. You made it right when you handed him the three dollars, and he forgave you when he accepted it. The nice part is you can now walk past his place, hold your head high, and be proud you did the correct thing. Nobody can ever take that away from you." Mama gave me a big hug and told me how proud she was that I had done the right thing.

# CHAPTER TEN

# Acting Out Imaginations

Summer vacation had arrived at last. I was able to sleep later in the mornings. Waking up sometimes would take thirty minutes or more. Outside the sun was shining bright, casting rays through the window across my bed. I would look up at the sun's rays, and I could see some dust particles floating lazily in the air. I imagined these particles to be a flock of birds leisurely flying in a circular pattern. Then I would pick up the corner of my sheet and move it up and down, creating some air turbulence. The particles would scurry around in much faster motion, just like a flock of birds did when frantically looking for shelter as it was starting to storm. I repeated this several times until the sun was higher in the sky. Then it no longer cast rays over the bed. That was when I knew I had to get up and eat some breakfast.

One day Mama said, "Shorty stopped by and picked up Papa." They were working on a barn six miles north of town.

Mike and I thought it would be a good day to play traveling cars. We went outside, and sure enough, Papa's car was sitting in the driveway.

Mike said, "We could have a lot of fun this morning just pretending we are going places in the car."

We got in the car, Mike behind the steering wheel and me on the passenger side. Mike said Papa told him all about how the car worked, so he figured he could handle the driving if I could be looking out for him. Mike explained to me about the clutch, and how you had to push it in when shifting gears and then let it out very slowly so the car would move smoothly. He said the brake pedal was for stopping. He liked to call the gas pedal the foot feed, because you had to operate it with your foot to control how much gas you were giving the engine.

He looked over at me and asked, "Are you ready to go?"

I said, "Let's get going."

So Mike pretended to turn the key and push the starter button. He began to make an *err-err-err* noise, as if the starter was trying to start the engine. Suddenly, he made a *brrumm* noise by blowing air out and letting his lips vibrate together.

He said, "I got the engine started. At first we will go real slow so we get used to it." He turned the steering wheel slowly clockwise about a quarter of a turn, then counterclockwise the same, and repeated this, as if we were moving. Soon he said, "We are on the open highway," and worked the steering wheel back and forth intensely. The faster we thought we were going, the faster he would turn the wheel.

Suddenly, I shouted, "Stop!"

He said, "We are coming to a screeching halt."

I said to Mike, "That was a close one. We just barely missed the train that is flying in front of us now." After we imagined the train had passed, we got started again on the open highway.

Suddenly, he started moving the steering fiercely and making the loud *brrumm* motor noise. He said, "We have to make up time, didn't plan on that train. Can you look and see just how fast we are going?"

I looked over at the speedometer and said, "It looks like we are going about a hundred and ninety-two miles per hour."

He said, "At this rate we'll be in New York City in about ten minutes."

I thought that New York City was a big place, and we'd see if he was a good driver. He got us right on through without any problems. I told him we had better get back home before it got too late.

He agreed and said, "We will get turned around and head that direction."

We had been making this trip for the last couple of hours, and I was getting hungry.

Mike said, "Well, here we are right at home."

I opened my door and stepped on the running board of the car. When my foot hit the ground, I knew I wasn't a captive of my imagination living in a fantasy world of make-believe any longer.

The car had stayed in the driveway. It had never moved. It was fun and we both were exhausted.

We ran in the house and Mama made us some lunch. She had just made rolls, making the house smell good. She took one of her freshly baked rolls and carefully cut it the long way, so now there were two nice slabs of bread. She spread some peanut butter on them, put them back together, and cut them in half, giving each of us a half. We devoured them in a flash. We went outside again so we could go downtown.

We took our time going downtown, trying to go in every back alley on the way. Scavenging for anything, we tried to find something that would capture our interest. It took us a couple of hours, but we finally wound up in the alley behind the café that was almost two miles from our house. When we got there, I spotted a couple of boys coming up the alley from the south end. It was the Watson brothers, Toby and Tom. We met them right behind the cafe.

They said they were messing around and looking for something exciting to do. Toby was about two years older than Tom, and he was a grade ahead of me in school.

He should have been two grades, but he had trouble and had to take one a second time. He got into trouble a lot and was full of mischief most of the time. Tom was more like me, always wanting to do the right thing. We talked about some of the things we could do to have fun. With four boys together and no supervision, there might be trouble brewing just around the corner. Doing something exciting was what we wanted.

Toby said, "I was messing around the grain elevator yesterday by the tractors and the old pickup truck. The elevator workers use the pickup when they move grain. They leave the key in it at night."

He thought it would be fun to take it for a drive. I was rather naïve and didn't think we would be making the truck move. Besides, none of us actually knew how to drive, but it was interesting to talk about it. We thought it would be exciting if we did take it for a drive.

Mike said, "We have to have a plan." Turning to Toby, he said, "Why don't you and Tom figure one? Billy and I will figure one, and then we will see which particular plan is the best and do it. That way, if someone or the cop comes, we will be able to get away without being caught."

I asked, "Does the cop ever check at night behind the elevator, where the tractors and truck are kept?"

Toby said, "Yes, he comes around about six o'clock."

The cop wasn't a very tall man and maybe just a little overweight. He was a jolly sort of fellow. When he laughed sometimes his belly would jiggle like a bowl of Jell-O. What he lacked in ambition he made up for with perseverance. His name was Wallace Andrews. Everyone called him Wally. Wally would always come to the scene. However, he was never the first one there. He liked to stay in his car most of the time.

Toby said, "Wally will come around again at ten or eleven. By that time we can have it out and back."

I asked, "Isn't this stealing?"

Mike said, "Billy, the pickup truck is now parked by the old tin shed. In the morning that is where it will be parked. So how can it be stolen, if it is still there?"

That sure sounded logical to me.

Mike asked, "Is there anyone who would rather stay home than go for a ride tonight?"

Of course, I knew what we were thinking of doing was probably wrong, but I wanted the adventure and wasn't going to raise any concerns if nobody else did. Besides, my heart was beating fast at just the thought of doing something that exciting.

Mike said, "Okay, then we should go home, eat supper, and meet down by the big elm tree near the elevator at seven o'clock."

Mike and I went home, and without saying anything to anybody, we ate our supper. We told Mama we were going outside to play.

Once outside we snuck past the old barn, then right along the broken-down fence to the south street. We quickly made our way to the meeting place down by the elevator. By the time we got there, the Watson brothers were already there.

Toby said, "Tom and I came down the main street, and we saw the police car parked in front of the cafe." We knew he would be there for quite a while. Once he shut the engine off, he couldn't get it started again because a vapor lock would constantly occur in the gas line, and he always had to wait about fifteen minutes before it would start. It took Wally at least an hour every time he stopped at the cafe. This would give us enough time to be able to go and come back before he would make another round.

Toby said, "I have already checked the pickup, and the keys are in it."

We talked over our plans and agreed Mike had the best one. We discussed who was most qualified to drive and thought Mike should be the one. We all ran over to the pickup, checking around as we went to see if anyone may might be looking.

Toby said, "It looks like we are about to have some real fun."

As I got in the truck, my pulse quickened and my heart was just pounding in my chest. The excitement of pulling off this caper was swirling around in my head. Everything up to that instant seemed to be captured in my imagination. Hearing the engine start and then feeling the truck move, I then knew taking it for a ride was real. I looked out the windshield, then out the back window, my eyes darting back and forth to make sure the area was clear of anyone who could identify us.

I gave the "all clear" to Mike. Instantly, Mike responded by pressing on the accelerator. Immediately, the truck lurched forward with a jerking motion, propelling me back in the seat. I looked out the side window and we were actually moving. We didn't go too far before Mike discovered that he didn't have to turn the steering wheel back and forth as much. That was a good thing, because it sure was uncomfortable sliding to the right and left sideways in the seat.

After shifting into second gear he headed south out of town, following the road as it made a curve to the east. It was so exciting—there we were, all four of us, speeding along in the country and just barely able to see out the windshield. I saw farmhouses along the way, each looking a little different. Most of them had a yard light on, mounted on top of a thirty-foot pole that when turned on would illuminate the yard area. It was good for farmers to have, because when they had visitors, they could turn it on to see who was coming and welcome them. I was watching the yard lights as we passed on the road.

Seeing them flickering through the tree leaves looked like flakes of tinsel twirling in the moonlight.

We stopped on a hill. Looking off to the left, there was a bunch of lights about a mile away.

Mike said, "I think it is a town named Everly."

Toby wanted to go down and find out.

Mike said, "We'll get caught for sure if we do, so we'd better turn around and head back home."

Going back, I noticed a lot of the farmhouses that had had yard lights on were now dark. That was an indication the farm family had gone to bed for the night. Then I realized it was late when we arrived at the elevator.

Mike said, "Let's park it before we get caught."

We spotted Wally's patrol car parked in the area where the pickup should be.

Mike said, "We'll turn off the lights before we turn in the driveway, and then we'll jump out and run. We know this area better than Wally."

So, with the truck still moving we jumped out and ran. The truck kept coasting slowly until it hit the side of an empty metal building, making a horrendous rattling noise, and then the engine stopped.

This may have startled Wally. He turned on his red lights and they flashed in the darkness. He turned on his siren. The high whining pierced the night air. Next, he turned on his spotlight, shining it right on the pickup truck. I could hear the roar of his engine; his car leaped forward as the back tires sprayed gravel and rock in the empty air behind him. His engine sputtered; he must have let the clutch out too quickly. He had stalled the engine of his patrol car. He shut off the red flashing lights. It was kind of an eerie feeling when he turned off his siren, with it coasting from a high-pitched whine to silence. He kept his spotlight focused on the truck. Maybe he thought at any moment someone was going to emerge from it.

We were hiding in the weeds. We knew we were safe after he stalled his engine because of the vapor lock problem. We decided to go home before we could get in any more trouble. So we separated and each of us headed home.

The next morning we got up and messed around outside for a while. Mike wanted to go to the corner gas station. After we got there, Mike told the station operator, Harry Jenkins, we wanted to buy a pouch of Red Man chewing tobacco. Of course Harry had to ask, "Who is it for?"

Right away Mike said, "It is for my dad."

I wondered how many times Harry had heard that before. Without any more hesitation, Harry took Mike's money and handed him a pouch.

As we were going out the door, Harry said, "I am going to check with your dad, do you boys hear?"

On the way back home, Mike opened the pouch, took some tobacco out and put it in his mouth. He handed the pouch to me, so I took a good-sized pinch between my thumb and forefinger just like the older guys downtown did and put it in my mouth. Immediately, I had the most awful taste in my mouth, but I wasn't going to spit it out. I started to chew just like I had seen the men do, and I even tried to spit like them. We were walking back home when we spotted Wally's patrol car turning the corner and coming in our direction. We both figured he was after us about the elevator pickup last night, so we started to run. I was doing really well. Then I tripped, and oops—I swallowed that wad of tobacco. Mike came back to where I lay to find out if I was hurt. I told him I accidently swallowed the tobacco.

He said, "Your face looks real pale, are you getting sick?"

I looked up and could see several of him. In fact, I could see several of everything. He held out his hand to help me, but I didn't know which one of the several I was seeing to reach for. I told him, "I feel real dizzy and faint."

Mike helped me up so he could get me home. He told Mama he thought I had the flu. Mama said, "Yes, it looks like it." She noticed something brown drizzling down my chin and the spots on my shirt. She said, "You don't see color like that, unless a person is terribly ill."

She felt my head and commented, "It may be the most awful case of 'boys growing up flu' I have ever seen. Probably, the only thing that will cure it is for Billy to swallow a couple of tablespoons of cod liver oil."

Suddenly, I began to feel better.

# CHAPTER ELEVEN

# At Grandma's House

Summer was going fast. It was already early August. Mama had to go back to the university hospital for her follow-up checkup. Since school was out for the summer, we kids had to stay with friends and relatives while she was gone. I thought I should tell Gramps, Bert, and Fred that I was going to be gone for maybe two weeks. "Don't expect me to come around and bug you because I am going to stay with my Grandma Oliver," I said.

Mike was going to stay with friends west of town. Tim would be staying with one of our aunts. I found out I would be staying with Grandma Oliver. I thought I had lucked out because Grandma was such a fine cook. You could tell by the way she looked that her cooking agreed with her. I was sure we would have good things to eat every day.

When I was taken to Grandma's house, the first thing she wanted me to do was take a bath. She said, "Billy, we need to get some of that dirt and grunge off you, so we can see what you really look like."

I knew Grandma had an indoor bathroom with a real bathtub in it, so I thought it would be okay if I took a bath. She filled the bathtub about half full of warm water and gave me instructions to get in and wash with soap all over. As soon as she left the bathroom I got into the tub. The water was warm and clean. I had never taken a bath in a real bathtub, so I was going to enjoy it.

I must have been in the tub about twenty-five minutes when I heard Grandma at the door, saying, "Billy, if you stay in there much longer you will be shriveled up like a prune. If you don't want to look like a prune, you better get out now."

I got out, dried off, and put on some clean clothes. When I left the bathroom, the first thing Grandma did was inspect to see how thorough of a job I did washing. She said it looked pretty good until she looked in my ears. Then she said, "Oh my goodness, I think we could grow potatoes in your ears. You forgot to wash them." She got a washcloth with some soap and water on it and put it over her index finger. She then put her finger in my ear and, with a twisting motion back and forth, she proceeded to wash my ear. It felt like she was trying to drill a hole in my head. When she got the first ear done, she did my other ear the same way. I thought the way she was digging and twisting, if she had done both ears at the same time she probably would have been able to touch her fingertips together right inside my head.

She said, "I have got them clean. I bet you will be able to hear a lot better now." I was glad she was done because I don't know if my ears could have stood any more of that kind of punishment. She said, "Now let's take a look at the bathtub." Everyone has heard about a ring around the tub. A ring around the tub had a new meaning after the water had drained. It was a dark ring. Grandma said, "I'll get the scouring powder, and together we will wash it clean so whoever is next to use it will have a spotless tub." We both worked and had to scrub in some spots to get it clean, and finally we were done.

Grandma said, "You sure don't look like the same boy. You look nice. Soon we will have some supper." When it came to food, I was always ready. She said, "We are going to have some ham and potatoes fried in fresh rendered lard, with sliced tomatoes from the garden and store-bought bread." I told her that really sounded good; another one of my favorite meals. She said, "Right after we get the dishes done, would you like to play cards?"

I said, "I don't know how to play any card games."

She asked me, "Would you like to learn how to play cards?" She thought the card game five hundred would be easy for me to learn.

I thought that would be fun, so I said, "Sure, I want to learn."

Grandpa said, "After we are done eating, you and I will do the dishes for Grandma. I will wash and you can dry, and in no time we will have them done."

Right after supper, Grandma was busy setting up the card table. Everything had to be just so. She wanted me to sit in front of the mirrored closet door, and Grandpa was to sit where he usually did, in front of a small table that had a mirror on the wall behind it. Grandma said she would sit facing both of us. We all sat where she wanted us to. She then explained how the game was played. We took out all the twos and threes, which left forty-four cards. When we add a joker, the deck totaled forty-five. She said, "You are supposed to play with four people, but since we only have three we will have what we call a dummy hand."

She said, "Billy, you and Grandpa will be partners and my partner will be the dummy hand." Then we dealt the cards, with each of us getting ten. There were five left over and that is what we called the kitty. We played auction bidding, which meant the bid kept going around the table until we had the highest bidder. The kitty went to the person who won the highest bid. They take the kitty, put it in their hand, and then discard any of the cards in their hand that they don't want.

The bidding started with the person to the left of the dealer. That person could either bid or pass. If that person bid, let's say, six hearts, and they got the bid, that team had to take at least six tricks. That was called, "They have made their bid." With some more explaining and some actual playing, I was beginning to catch on to how the game was played. Grandpa helped me keep score. He said there was so much to learn, and it took time. We played a few practice hands, and I made a few bids. We won some, and we lost some. That is what Grandpa wanted me to do so I would know how the game was played.

Grandma said, "Okay, it is time to play some real cards. Now this is for keeps. We will see which team is the best, whether it is me and the dummy or Grandpa and Billy." With Grandpa sitting to Grandma's left, he was the first bidder, and he said, "Eight clubs."

The one next to Grandpa was the dummy hand. Since the dummy couldn't talk, it was my turn. I looked at my cards and thought there was no way I could take five tricks, so I passed. Then it was Grandma's turn. She looked in my direction, then in Grandpa's direction, and said, "Eight hearts."

Grandpa said to her, "It's yours. Hearts will be trump. The bid is too high for us." Grandma got the kitty, took what she wanted and discarded what she didn't. Next, she picked up the dummy hand, and I could see that she was rearranging it before she put it down again.

Then it was my turn to start, so I threw out the six of spades. She played the top one of the dummy's hands, and it was a heart, which was trump. Grandpa had to follow with a spade and so did Grandma, but since the dummy hand trumped the trick, they won it.

This went on for the rest of the night. I think we only got the bid four other times, and Grandma set us three of those four. Grandma won every game we played, and after a win she would whoop it up and carry on with a little dance behind her chair.

Soon it was time for me to go to bed. Grandpa said, "Get a good night's sleep, because I want you to help me wash some bottles tomorrow. We will use those bottles for tomato juice."

Next morning for breakfast we had scrambled eggs, fried potatoes, pork cracklings (the remains Grandma had from rendering lard), toast, and tomato juice. I told Grandma that meal was one of my favorites.

Right after breakfast, Grandpa washed the dishes and I dried. Grandpa said we needed to go down in the basement to wash bottles because Grandma wanted to preserve some tomato juice later in the week.

Grandpa had a bottle of Grain Belt Beer three or four times a week. He would save the bottles because they were clear. We had a lot of those bottles to wash, so

Grandpa rigged up a method that worked pretty slick. He had a soft-bristle bottle brush with a long handle on it. He made a block of wood with a hole drilled clear through it. On one side of the block he drilled a bigger hole, about the size of a bottle neck, using the smaller hole as a guide, but he didn't drill clear through. He put the long handle of the brush through the small hole and had it bent to look like a crank. Now he could push the soft bristle end in the bottle with the wooden block fitting pretty good on the bottle opening. He could hold the block of wood and the bottle at the same time while using his other hand to turn the crank, which did a nice job of scrubbing the inside of the bottle. It was my job to take the bottle when he was done cleaning it, rinse it, and set it on the rack upside down to dry.

We were about half done when Grandpa said, "You know, Billy, there are just four things about cards that can get Grandma going. She loves to win or loves to set the other team. This causes her to want to whoop it up. She hates losing or just having the other team make their bid. This causes her to be real quiet and clam up. The only time Grandma cheats is when she thinks she can win."

I said, "She won every game last night. Does that mean she cheated every game?"

Grandpa said he didn't know, but he thought it was time to teach her a lesson. He said, "You hold your cards in your right hand. When holding your left hand down on your lap, if you have an ace, hold your cards with one finger showing on the back side of your cards. If you have two aces, have two fingers show. If you have three aces, have three fingers show. Now, if you have a king, then put your left hand up on the table and do the same as you did with the aces. That should help me have some advantage over her."

We finished washing the bottles, and it was time for lunch. Grandma had some cold chicken left from Sunday's dinner; I told her that was one of my favorites. In the afternoon Grandpa and I picked tomatoes. We had them everywhere in the house that we could find a flat spot to put them. We even had some piled on the back porch.

I was tired from helping Grandpa all day. I asked Grandma if I could take a bath. She looked kind of puzzled and said, "Bath two days in a row, when you probably haven't had two all this year? It will make you feel good for supper and you sure will sleep soundly tonight."

Right after we finished supper and the dishes, we went in the front room to play cards. I understood how to play five hundred. I just wished I could win once in a while. All five of the games we played Grandma won. I did exactly like Grandpa told me to do, but we always got beat.

Next morning after breakfast, we started washing the tomatoes in clean pails of water outside to prepare them for Grandma to juice. Grandpa and I were busy washing when he said, "We lost again last night. We can't even cheat and win. Grandma won them all. I guess she must be cheating better than what we can."

I said, "Grandma is just sitting in a lucky chair. Tonight I want to sit there, and you sit where the dummy hand is. Maybe that will change our luck."

We would take the clean tomatoes in for Grandma to cut up and cook in a big kettle. When they had reached the right temperature, she would dip them out of the kettle and put them through a fine-screen colander. This would result in some good-looking tomato juice. Grandma would then add salt to make it taste right.

After the juice cooled a little, Grandpa would put a funnel in the bottles we had just washed. He poured in a dipper full and repeated this until it was filled up to where the neck of the bottle started. He would then put a bottle cap on each one, and with a tool he had he would crimp the cap to make it seal.

Grandma would then put them in a warm water bath. She would turn the gas burner up a little to get the water higher in temperature. That would expand the air in the neck, causing it to be pushed out under the seal. When the water reached the right temperature, she would retrieve the full bottle with a special tool made for lifting bottles by the neck and set them on a piece of wood Grandpa had made just the size of the table. He said,

"That way, the bottles don't get a temperature shock."
There they would cool and completely seal, creating a
small vacuum in the air space in each bottle. When you
would open one with a bottle opener you could hear a
*psss* sound, just like when you opened a bottle of pop.

Since the table was full of bottled tomato juice,
Grandma said we would eat our supper outside on the
back lawn. We would have a picnic and there would be
less to clean up after supper, but we had to bring everything back in the house.

After supper, we just had to play some cards, and I
wanted to sit in the lucky chair where Grandma sat. So
we moved around the table like I had suggested. We
did finally win a game. Grandma was very quiet and
had already, as Grandpa said, "clammed up." I noticed
Grandma was sitting where I sat the night before. It
looked kind of funny because I also could see her in the
mirror behind her.

After breakfast the next morning, we went out to
the garage by the alley. Grandpa kept his 1926 Model
T there. About once a week he would open the garage
door and back his beloved car out of the garage. He
could no longer drive because of health reasons. He
would spend the next couple of hours wiping all the dust
off it. When he had it running outside I thought it sure
sounded funny compared to Papa's. I asked Grandpa
if I could blow the horn, and he said not more than

twice or the neighbors might complain. So I pushed the horn button. It scared me to hear a loud *ah-ooga*. I did it again; another *ah-ooga*. Grandpa said that was enough. We had to put the Ford back in the garage.

After Grandpa got the Ford back in the garage, he and I got to talking about the card games the previous night. I said, "We finally won a game, and that was because I was sitting in the lucky chair." I told him the back of his head looked funny when he was studying his cards.

He asked, "How could you see that when you were right across the table from me?"

I told him I could see him in the mirror behind him.

He then asked, "Could you see Grandma, too?"

I said, "I sure could, and everything looked backward when looking at it in the mirror."

He said, "Billy, I think you have just discovered how Grandma can win all the time. She can see what you have in the mirror behind you. She then looks to see what I have in the mirror behind me. She looks at the dummy hand and rearranges it, and even gets the kitty to pick the cards she wants. You know she has looked and knows where every single card is. No wonder she can win all the time."

I looked kind of surprised, and asked Grandpa, "Would Grandma cheat that much?"

He said, "When it comes to playing cards, Grandma likes to win more than anything. We won't let her know that we have figured out how she does it. Tonight we will sit back in the same places we sat in the first night. Only this time when we are dealt, we will hold our cards close to our chest. That way, she won't be able to see our hands in the mirror. Billy, you use the same signals for aces and kings, just like we had talked about."

After supper, we went in the front room to play cards. I remembered everything Grandpa told me, and sure enough, we won the first game. Then we won the second, and the third. I could see it was bothering Grandma that she hadn't won. She did win the fourth game, but we won the fifth.

Then Grandpa said to Grandma, "We have figured out how you could win all the time. You can look in the mirror behind each one of us and see what cards we have in our hands. You always get the bid, so you get the kitty, too. Now you know where every card in the deck is so you can play accordingly. That is cheating. You know it, and now we know it. That is teaching Billy to do wrong. I have told him some stuff about how to let me know what he has in his hand and I was wrong doing that. Billy wanting to sit in your chair is how we finally figured out that you were cheating."

I could see Grandma getting red in the face; it almost looked like fire coming from her eyes right through her wire-rimmed glasses. I could see her lips quivering, and she nearly had steam coming out of her ears. She looked really guilty and very upset. That was when Grandma said, "It is time to go to bed." I could see Grandpa snickering. He enjoyed catching Grandma cheating.

The next morning after breakfast, Grandma said, "Billy, I am sorry I cheated playing cards. I got so caught up in the moment. I just want to win more than anything."

I said, "Maybe we should move the card table away from the mirrors and all of us play by the rules."

"That sounds like a good idea," Grandma said.

As soon as Grandpa and I were done with dishes, I went with Grandma into the living room to watch her crochet. I was amazed at how she could take one strand of thread, along with a crochet hook; do some poking, twisting, hooking, turning, looping, and pulling tight; and have it create the most beautiful lace doily I had ever seen. I was fascinated by all the movement. I even looked at the directions she was following. I sure didn't know what they meant, no matter if I looked at them right side up or upside down.

In the afternoon, I watched Grandma make a chocolate cake. After she got done mixing the batter, she poured it in a pan. Using her spatula, she scraped the mixing bowl almost clean, leaving just a little spot for me. Using my finger, I wiped some batter and stuck it in my mouth. Of course it tasted good, causing me to smack my lips. Soon I had the bowl licked clean.

Grandma said, "We are going to have the cake after supper and listen to the Great Gildersleeve on the radio." I thought maybe Grandma was making the cake to try to butter us up, so she could win playing cards.

My stay with Grandma came to an end all too soon. Papa and Mama returned home quicker than originally planned. Mama had her follow-up checkup at the hospital and was released right away. She was told there was nothing more they could do. Mama told them she would just have to hope for a miracle. I could tell Mama was weaker than before she went.

I got in the car, I told Grandma good-bye and we started for home. When we got there it was a welcome sight for Mama. She said she had to lie down and rest for a while. I was worried about Mama. With school so close to starting, I honestly didn't know what I would do. Mama always had clean clothes and lunches ready for us when we started back to school. I could sense this year would be different.

# CHAPTER TWELVE

# Comforting Mama

With only a couple of days before school started, I wanted to use my time wisely. I thought I would like to see what, if anything, happened while I was at Grandma's house. I saw Gramps working in his garden, wearing the ever-present cap that was round and flat on top. I went over to see what he was doing. It looked like he was digging potatoes. He gave me a small one and said, "Rub the dirt off, put some salt on it, and eat it. This year they taste good." I did and, sure enough, it was pretty tasty. I told him I was going to Fred and Bessie's. I wanted to see if Fred was going to his farm because I wanted to see the squirrels. I had made friends with one that had a hurt hind leg, and I wanted to see how it was doing.

I went from Gramps's place south past Dr. Redman's. At first I thought I might be uneasy about walking by, but I soon found out I was proud of myself. I held my head high. I knew then I had done the right thing.

I arrived at Fred and Bessie's just in time. They were dressed up and about to get in their car. I was as glad to see them as they were to see me. Fred said, "We have to go to a funeral. Why don't you come over tomorrow?"

I told him, "That sounds like a plan. I'll be back tomorrow."

From Fred's, I walked past the school. After all, I felt as if I should check the area out. To my surprise, I found they had built a building on the corner of the school yard. It had doors and windows in it. I couldn't get inside to look around because the men were still working on it. It had just the black weather paper on the outside held on by long narrow thin strips of wood. I could see they were going to put siding on it and probably paint it before winter. I wished I knew what it was going to be.

On the way home, I had to go past Bert's. I saw him working in his yard, and hollered, "Hi!"

He looked up and said, "Billy, you are home already. I have been looking forward to seeing you again. I have to tell you about my fishing experiences while you were gone."

I went over and sat down beside Bert. I just loved to hear him tell stories. He said he was out fishing the week before, kind of dozing off a bit, when it felt like his fishing pole was about to be jerked out of his hand. He said that woke him up. He knew he had a fish on his line, but didn't know how big. He gestured like he was straining, holding his rod and trying to crank the reel at the same time. I caught myself doing a similar thing. He said first that fish would dart on this side of the boat—he looked to his left, and I did the same—then it would dart to the other side of the boat—he looked to his right, and again I copied him. He said that monster continued to do that for almost an hour. Finally, he got it in the boat. It was huge, but he had to throw it back because it had used a lot of energy in the great battle with him and as a result lost weight. He said, "It was so thin you could almost look through it from the side." I thought, *Wow. I would like to see a fish that large.* I was sitting there with big eyes and my mouth open. I couldn't imagine a fish that large. I knew it was true because Bert said it was.

Starting back to school was different that year. Mike and Tim had already gone ahead of me. I had to wear the best-looking overalls and shirt I had. Mama was sick and unable to do the washing or make any new shirts. I was confused as to how we were going to have clean clothes and lunches.

When I got to school, I walked past the new building on the corner of the school yard. I went into my classroom, and immediately my teacher sent me to the principal's office. When I got there, Mike and Tim were already there. I looked at them and they looked at me. Then I asked, "What is going on?" They didn't know any more than I did of what was going to happen.

Soon, the principal came in and said, "I called you boys in here so I can tell you all about what the town committee wants to do for you. They know how sick your mother is and would like to help so you will be able to proudly attend school. They have bought enough school supplies for each of you. Right after school today, you boys go to the clothing store. The committee has bought each of you some clothes and new shoes. That new building on the corner of the school yard is the new hot-lunch building. The town committee has bought each of you a hot-lunch ticket so you will be able to eat a hot lunch with the rest of the kids."

Right after school we went to the clothing store. The clerk had a package for each of us to take home. I hurried home, as I wanted to show Mama what was in my package. Both Mike and Tim arrived home before I did, and they put their packages upstairs in our bedroom and went outside to play.

When I got home, I found Mama sitting by the north window looking out. I could see the hopelessness in her face. I asked, "Mama, what is wrong?"

She said, "I just want to see you kids grow up and be healthy. I think maybe I have seen you as far as I am capable of. I want you kids to go to school, learn, and get good jobs."

I said, "I want to show you what the town committee bought us today." But first, I wanted to tell her about the hot-lunch tickets the town committee bought us. "We can eat hot lunch every day, free, by using these tickets.

Today we had macaroni and cheese with carrots and celery sticks, and a bread and butter sandwich with milk. It was one of my favorites. One kid sitting beside me didn't like his, so I ate it, too. Now I want to show you what is in my package." I opened it and showed her the clothes and shoes.

She looked at them and said, "My prayers have been answered. I am grateful for charity. Aunt Nellie and her husband Fred stopped in with Grandma Planter today. It took them a while to get Grandma in the house, but she wanted to see me before she went home with Aunt Nellie." Grandma was now going to live with Aunt Nellie, Mama's older sister, because she couldn't take care of herself very well anymore. Mama looked at me and said, "Billy, please help me back to bed to lie down."

I could see how sick Mama was, and it made me very sad. Mama loved flowers, so I decided to pick her a nice bouquet of wild roses, hoping that would cheer her up. Going outside and looking in the roadside ditch rewarded me with some beautiful flowers. Maybe this would make Mama feel better. Taking them in the house to show Mama made me feel a lot better.

She sort of smiled when she saw them, and gave me a big hug and said, "Billy, you are so thoughtful, and very special to me. Plants will tell us a story if we let them. Look at the flowers you just picked. Can you see the sturdy, straight stems? They represent how we should live our lives. We want to grow up healthy and strong. The thorns and stickers on the stem tell us to be careful and protect ourselves. Look at the nice green leaves, they represent life experiences, like when worthy things happen, like when you are going to school, listening to the teacher, studying and getting excellent grades, and wanting to learn more. If some of the leaves are green with a little russet-colored edge around them, it still could be reasonable things happening to you, like going to school, and maybe you didn't study as hard and didn't get the best grade you could. Look and see leaves that have turned a dark brown color. That says you are not applying yourself, not studying, and not getting the knowledge out of school like you should. Look at the beautiful blossoms, they represent love and respect. Look at the white rose, with its petals tightly wrapped into a small pointed bud. It represents purity and innocence. First you must love and respect yourself before you can love and respect anyone else. There are two types of respect: the kind of respect you earn, and the kind of respect you command. You earn respect of your body by giving it food and water so it will respond to the tasks you desire. You earn respect from others by saying please and thank you, and sharing. Demanding respect is when you eat or drink something that is not good for you, and you want your body to function the same as if you gave it good food and something good to drink. Demanding respect from others is when you say, *'gimme, gimme, gimme,'* and then take everything without acknowledging anyone else is there. Billy, the best kind of respect is the kind you earn. People don't ever forget that kind. Just remember, earned respect is everlasting, and demanded respect is momentary. You have love when you fill your spirit with belief, like going to Sunday school and doing to others the way you would like to have them do to you. You know, Billy, if everyone in the world had that kind of love and respect, there wouldn't be any crime, and there wouldn't be any wars. This would be such a wonderful place to live. Look down here, on the side, there is a bud. That is a bloom that hasn't opened yet. Those buds represent hope and promise. The children of the world are the hope and promise for all future generations, and you are part of that."

I had picked the flowers to cheer Mama up. She had such a neat way of expressing and explaining things that made them very easy for me to understand. At that very moment, I felt the sadness I had was gone. I felt a lot better. I wanted to hug Mama; I had to be careful, and went to her right side because her surgery was on the left side of her chest. I walked around to the right side and give Mama the biggest hug I could. She understood. I brought flowers in order to cheer her up, and she had done her best to cheer me up and make me feel better. Mama was so special to me.

Each day when I got home from school, I would water and check Mama's flowers. If I saw one that looked like it was on its last legs, I would take it out and replace it with a new one. I continued this until I couldn't find any more that were blooming.

That year the fall seemed longer than other years. We didn't have any potatoes to dig or vegetables canned. With Mama so sick that summer, those kinds of chores just didn't get done.

On the first Saturday after school started for the year, I got up early and went outside. I walked down by Highway 18 and saw the Colonial Bread truck (all their trucks had "Colonial is good bread" painted on the side) stop at the corner of our street and the highway. The driver backed the truck off the highway and around the corner onto our street, and stopped. I was close by and I saw him get out and go to the back of his truck.

I went over and told him I was Billy Oliver. Then I asked him, "What is your name, and what are you doing?"

He said his name was Sam, and he was rearranging his load by putting all the empty bread racks on top of his truck. He said I could help by handing the empty racks up to him, so he could put them on top of his truck. I found the racks weren't heavy, so I could handle them easily. When we had put all the empty racks on top of his truck, Sam gave me a package of day-old Danish pastry.

He said he was returning it from a store, so he gave it to me for helping him.

I took the Danish pastry home to share with Mike and Tim. We opened the package and each of us took one.

Mike said, "What if they took the glob of jam off?"

Tim said, "What if they took all the sweet frosting off?"

I said, "All that would be left would be rolls."

At that point, we all agreed that what was left sure didn't taste like what Mama made.

In late October, early on a Saturday morning, I went over to Fred and Bessie's. I wanted to be with someone who understood how I felt. I knew Mama was very sick. She rested better when it was quiet around the house. I wanted to have someone to talk to. I told Bessie about Mama being so sick; she could see my sadness.

She said, "Why don't you go with Fred out to the farm and pick up some corn for my squirrels? When you get back, I will have a nice apple pie baked, then you and Fred can enjoy a piece."

I liked that idea, so I waited for Fred to get Jim and Joe hitched to the wagon and two five-gallon cream cans filled with water. Then Fred motioned for me to get on the wagon.

He said, "We only need two cans of water today for the horses. It is cool, and we won't be out at the farm

for more than a couple of hours. I am glad you are coming along. We're going to pick up corn that fell on the
ground before the corn picker could pick it. Bessie loves
it when I bring home whole ears of corn. She likes to
feed and watch the squirrels in the wintertime. Since
we don't have any nut trees in our yard, the squirrels
depend on her."

I got on the wagon right beside Fred and he made
that *click-click* out the side of his mouth. Jim and Joe
started forward. The harness became tight, and then we
were moving. Once we got out on the road, the horses
moved into a rhythmic clip-clop trot. Fred and I chatted
the whole way, and soon we were at his farm. Fred set the
cans of water near a big oak tree.

He said, "We will have the horses pull the wagon
through the field, and when we spot an ear on the
ground, we will throw it in the wagon." We made several
passes through the field and claimed the fallen ears.
Fred looked at the nice pile of corn in the wagon box
and said, "That will be enough for Bessie's squirrels for
the winter." We gave Jim and Joe a drink of water and
then started home. I was tired and thirsty.

When we arrived at Fred's home, we put the corn we
found into a shed by the barn. We put the horses in the
barn and fed them. Now it was time to enjoy a piece of
Bessie's apple pie. We went into the house. There, Bessie
had a nice piece of pie and a glass of milk for me and pie

and coffee for Fred. The pie was very good. I told Bessie it was my favorite, then I thanked her and told them both it was kind of them to invite me. It helped me focus on happier thoughts. However, it was now time for me to go home.

Soon it was Thanksgiving. Again this year, we would go to Grandma Oliver's. Mama said she would stay home; she didn't feel well enough to go. When we arrived at Grandma's, I could smell all the good food. However, it wouldn't be the same since Mama couldn't come with us.

I ate slowly. I couldn't stop thinking of Mama. That is when I asked Grandma if she would fix something for Mama to eat, and we would take it to her. We left Grandma's earlier than usual. We brought Mama some of all the good things we had to eat. She thought that was nice and tried to eat some. I saw she was having a hard time swallowing. However, she did thank me for bringing some of Grandma's good food.

# CHAPTER THIRTEEN

# *Final Goodbye*

Christmas would soon be here. There was a lot of snow on the ground, and it was cold in the mornings. I would get out from under the warm, comfy covers on my bed and get dressed. It sure didn't take me very long to put on my clothes and get downstairs by the stove that was radiating cozy heat. Papa had gotten up earlier and had a nice glowing fire going in the stove.

We had a very small, beautiful Christmas tree at school. Our class had decorated it with tinsel, strings of popcorn, and a decorative paper chain. The chain was made of colored construction paper. We had cut it into strips and glued the ends together to make circles connecting to each other to make a chain. Our teacher, Mrs. Caps, said the janitor told her we had to put the tree outside before we went home for the holidays. It was so beautiful, just the thought of setting the tree outside with no one around to enjoy it made me sad. So I asked Mrs. Caps if I could have the tree to take home. She agreed, and then she helped me take off the decorative paper chain we made and put it in a sack so I could carry it.

As soon as school let out that day, I got the tree and started to carry it home in my left hand. It was a small tree, but after a short distance it got heavy, so I switched to my right hand, and continued to do this until I arrived home. I just had to show Mama how beautiful it looked.

Mama was very sick and had to be in bed all the time. She looked at the tree and told me how nice it looked, and said I should set it up by the wall farthest from the stove so that if it was dry, it wouldn't catch fire. I was hoping it would make Mama feel better that we finally had a Christmas tree. I even got to decorate it with the paper chain we made at school.

That year was different from years past. We had a Christmas tree, but there would be no presents. I thought it would be present enough if Mama could be with us on Christmas Day.

Just a day before Christmas, Mama was very sick and unable to lift her head off the pillow. Dr. Cash made a house call to see how Mama was doing. He saw how nauseous she was, so he advised Papa that he would authorize admitting her to the hospital. Papa was to take her there right away.

The morning of the second day after Christmas, Papa got home from the hospital and came in the house. I knew by the look on his face that something had happened. He had us boys sit down so he could explain that Mama had passed away just a few hours before and now was with baby Ray and the angels.

I cried out, "This is a terrible belated Christmas present!"

Then, suddenly, it felt like I was lying down and totally relaxed. I felt all the awareness and energy leaving my body, making it limp and unable to feel the emptiness. I was motionless. Then my mind went totally blank, and I could feel that awful hurt in my heart. It is as close to being mummified as I could ever describe. I stayed in that condition for the next two days. That time was the most painful reminder of Mama's absence that I had ever experienced. It seemed as if Mama was so real. She was here a few days ago. It wasn't clear to me what life would be like without Mama. Mama's acts of kindness and the love for me I would never be able to repay.

Then Papa asked if we wanted to go see Mama. He would take us. I saw how distraught he was over losing Mama just by the look on his face. He walked around in a daze, without a known destination or purpose in mind, just wandering. I saw how much he missed Mama, too.

When I went into the funeral home, I could see Mama. The stress, worry, and despair were gone from her face. She looked like she was at peace; she looked beautiful. Flowers were everywhere. They were red, pink, purple, and white, and there were so many.

After we had been there for a period of time, Papa said, "It is time for us to go. I will take you home now."

I turned to Papa and asked, "Could I be with Mama alone for a little while?"

He knew how close I was to Mama. He said, "Sure." He didn't want to deprive me of that one last experience with Mama.

With everyone out of the room I started talking out loud. There were several things I wanted to let Mama know, like how much I treasured her words of wisdom. I said, "Mama, remember last year when Fred and Bessie gave me a birthday cake? Bessie told me if I made a wish and blew out all the candles it might come true. The only one I have ever told is you, today, but my wish at that time was for you to feel better.

"Remember the time I told you about giving the three dollars that I had earned mowing Fred's lawn to Dr. Redman? It was to repay his daughter for the money we took. I made it right with myself and forgave myself. I was truthful with Dr. Redman. He accepted the money, so in a way he did forgive me. The nice part is I can walk past his place with my head held high and not feel guilty.

"I told you about writing some nasty words on Bert Miller's sidewalk with chalk. At first I was going to run just like all the other boys did. I started to, but then I stopped. I turned around. I knew we had done wrong. I went back to Bert and apologized, and offered to scrub off all the colorful words we wrote. I even made him my new friend.

"I will always remember you telling me how the respect that is earned is everlasting. The respect that is demanded will be only momentary.

"There is still one thing that is bothering me. I am telling you now for the first time. This past summer a group of us boys took the elevator's pickup truck for a ride one night. We took it way out in the country and then brought it back. I knew it was stealing. I didn't want to do it, but I got caught up in the excitement, and before I knew it I was right in the middle of it. Now that I have told you, it makes me feel a lot better about it.

"I remember you telling me how plants will tell us a story if we are wise enough to picture and think about it. Mama, look at all the flowers. The stems are straight and strong, just like you said we were to live our lives. See how green and lush the leaves are, representing life's experiences? See all the beautiful blossoms representing love?"

I reached over to a vase and pulled a white rosebud from it, and I then placed it upon her chest.

"I remember you telling me how the white buds that have not opened represent how life can be innocent and pure, and bring the promise of a new day."

With my heart heavy with hurt and sadness, I began to feel my legs wobbling. Then I thought I could hear Mama say, "Be strong, Billy." I had cried so much I thought there couldn't be any more liquid left in my body to shed another tear. But still my eyes started to fill with tears, to where they started to run down my cheeks. I had a lump in my throat and could hardly swallow. I knew that time would pass and memories would fade. But the experiences, the companionship, and the love I had for Mama would always be etched in my heart.

At that very moment, I knew I had lost my mama, my best friend.

I bowed my head and softly whispered, "Good-bye, Mama."

# CHAPTER FOURTEEN

# *Living with Grandma*

I was nine years old. I was confused and surprised. Seeing all the people who came to Mama's last gathering to pay their respects was overwhelming. Right away I saw Fred and Bessie in the third row back, and next to them were Bert and Grace. I looked around the room some more and could see Norm Willis in the back row. For me to see that many people who cared, or at least pretended they cared, was a humbling experience. I could tell which ones really cared. They were the ones that stayed around after the service wanting to know if they could help or do anything for us. Those that pretended to care were gone right after the service. Needless to say, there weren't very many who were sincere.

I wondered what would happen next. I had lost my mama. I had lost my best friend. Where was I to go, where would I sleep and eat? Was Papa going to abandon me now, too?

When some of the people started to leave, Papa got us kids together. He told us, "You will be going home with Aunt Sarah and Uncle Jacob. You kids will stay with them for three or four weeks. I need some time to get my affairs straightened out."

At that moment in time, I didn't know I would never see that old house we called home again. I wouldn't ever see all the neat things we had found and stored in the barn.

By no means would I ever see any part of my thousand-piece horse puzzle again.

Uncle Jacob and Aunt Sarah, Papa's younger sister, lived on a farm near a small town by Spencer. I thought that might be all right. I had never been on a farm, and it would be fun to learn about farm animals. Three of Aunt Sarah's kids had grown and left home. She had a couple of bedrooms that we could use while we stayed at her house. She said, "The first thing we have to do in the morning is to get you registered at school. You are only going to be staying for three or four weeks."

I think she liked the idea of us being in school because she could have some peace and quiet during the day. We would stay current in our schooling and wouldn't get behind.

My first day at school was quite an experience. I got to meet all the kids, but I wasn't very talkative. I sort of kept to myself. After all, I had just gone through a life-changing experience that was very vivid in my memory. It had happened so recently that it still seemed very real.

When we ate hot lunch, we would take our filled plates and half-pint bottles of milk to the gymnasium to eat. I had heard some people talking about how the gym was a cracker box in size. I didn't know what they meant until I went there to eat my lunch. It sure looked tiny to me. I did get to see a basketball game, looking down from the balcony seats. I could see the floor when our team took the court. It looked busy, and when the other team joined our team on the floor it looked crowded. I need to explain a bit about the gym area. With the gym being so small, the basketball court's black boundary line was painted just three inches from the wall on one side and on one end. When playing a game, there was no way for a player to stand outside the court boundaries, so they were allowed to stand on the line and throw the ball in play. During the game, if the ball hit the wall it was out of bounds.

On one side there were bleachers for people to watch basketball games. On one end was the stage for school plays and other events. Just above was the balcony, which was the second floor. Mounted on the edge of the balcony, overlooking the gym floor, was a foot-wide plank that was used as a table, with picnic-table seating attached. There was also a row of bleacher seats on the south side. This is where we ate our hot lunch.

The backboards with the basketball hoops attached were mounted to the wall with bracing connected to the balcony bracing. I could see the balcony tables shake and vibrate when the kids on the gym floor would shoot basketballs.

How in the world was I going to keep my plate of tuna and noodle casserole, one of my favorites, and glass half-pint bottle of milk from falling off? So I decided to watch other kids to see how they did it before I sat down. I could see they held onto their plate with one hand and their milk with the other. They would wait until there was a lull in shooting of basketballs toward the hoop, and then would take a forkful of food as fast as lightning, put it in their mouth, and just as quick hold on to their plates again.

That looked easy enough, so I sat down and tried it. Being left-handed, I held everything opposite the other kids. I was holding my half-pint bottle of milk in my left hand. I waited and found my opportunity. I left my milk sitting, grabbed my forkful of food, and put it in my mouth as fast as I could. Quickly, my hand returned to where I thought my milk was. I had just knocked my milk over the edge, and it broke on the gym floor below, making a huge mess. After that, I decided to eat my lunch on the bleacher seats behind us. I just could not get into the habit of gobbling my food that way.

When I got back to the farm after school, I went outside to be with Uncle Jacob while he did chores. First we went to the chicken house; I watched the chickens walk around singing *cluck-cluck-cluck*. I figured that strutting, singing, and scratching the floor were what chickens were supposed to do. Even the rooster was strutting around crowing.

I even got to see some of those hens lay eggs. The eggs the hens laid were white-shelled and brown-shelled. These were big, fat, old hens, just like the "fat old hen" that Grandma used for her Thanksgiving dinner of noodles and dumplings.

After a while I went over to the barn, and I saw Uncle Jacob feeding the cows hay and grain. It sure looked like the cows liked it. Then I watched Uncle Jacob milk the cows. That was the first time I had ever seen that. Up to then I had no idea where the milk we bought in the store came from. Give the cow some grain and hay on the front end, then go around toward the back and start pulling on those four little things hanging down, and magic happens. You get milk.

I had to ask Uncle Jacob, "What happens if you give the cow more hay and grain? Do you get more milk? If you make the chickens eat more feed, do they lay more eggs? Why are some eggs white and others are brown?"

Uncle Jacob laughed and said, "Billy, you are full of questions, and I will try to answer them. First, a cow will only give so much milk. Some breeds are for beef and some are for dairy. Some dairy farmers do give a little more grain and hay to their cows, and they do produce a little more. I am not trying to see how much milk I get. I just want to get enough for our use.

"Did you see the rooster strutting around crowing? He is always bragging to his lady hen friends, but they don't pay too much attention to him. As far as the chickens, it depends on the breed of chicken as to which lays white-shelled or brown-shelled eggs. Usually white chickens lay white-shelled eggs and darker-colored chickens lay brown-shelled eggs. There is no difference in nutritional value of the different-colored eggs as far as I know. Sometimes you will find yolks lighter or darker in color, and that depends on what the chicken eats. Oats and wheat cause light yolks, and corn causes darker yolks.

"The number of eggs a chicken can lay in one day is limited. Just because you force them to eat more it doesn't mean they will start laying eggs like a machine gun. Forcing chickens to eat more feed will only cause them to get fatter. They need time to scratch in the dirt and time to strut and sing."

I said, "You told me white eggs come from white chickens, brown eggs usually come from darker-colored chickens. Why is milk always white no matter if it comes from a black cow or a white cow?"

Uncle Jacob just chuckled and said, "Milk is rich in calcium, which is white. In addition, the cream found in the milk contains white-colored fat. Calcium and vitamin D are the two ingredients of milk that makes it very healthy for us to drink."

I would spend as much time as I could after school outside with Uncle Jacob. Everywhere he went, I tagged along. I was trying my hardest not to think about Fred and Bessie or Bert. Those were my two favorite places to go when I was home. I wanted to stay busy until we ate supper and then go to bed. Every night I said a prayer for Mama. I really missed her.

Soon three weeks passed, and it was time for Papa to decide where we kids would be going to live in a more permanent situation. Papa was there, along with Aunt Sarah, Grandma Oliver, and my oldest brother Lee. They were all gathered around the kitchen table as if they had a treasure chest full of gold and were about to divvy it up among them. At that point Grandma took over. She always did kind of rule the roost, so to speak.

Grandma called us kids into the kitchen and instructed each of us to write our names on the same-size pieces of paper she had cut up and put them in the hat in the center of the table. Grandma said, "I want this drawing to be fair. Whoever draws a name, then that youngster will go live with you." I wrote my name on the paper, and then I made a small fold on one corner of it before I put it in the hat. Grandma took the hat and shook it to mix up the names. She always went first, so she reached in and got a piece of paper with a name on it. Aunt Sarah, Lee, and Papa did the same thing. It was their way of deciding which one of us kids would be going with whom for a more permanent living arrangement.

Right away, I could see Aunt Sarah had my name from that little bent corner. I thought that would be okay with me, I sort of liked it on the farm. I could be around the animals and watch Uncle Jacob take care of them. Maybe I would get to help him. Just the thought of being on the farm was exciting for me.

Then Grandma said, "I have an announcement. I want everyone to put the names back in the hat because the drawing we just had was for practice only. I just wanted to see if everything was going to run smoothly." Everyone rolled his or her eyes and reluctantly put the slips of paper back in the hat. Once again, Grandma shook it and was first to draw a piece of paper out. Before anyone else drew, Grandma said, "This time it is for real." Immediately, I could see she had drawn a piece of paper that had a bent corner. I knew that was my paper. I knew then I would be going to live with Grandpa and Grandma Oliver. That was okay with me because Grandma always made good things to eat and knew what my favorites were. I would even get to play five hundred with her and Grandpa.

Each one who drew a name announced who he or she would be taking home. Everybody started talking and laughing, and then I heard Lee say, "We would be practicing until nightfall so Grandma could get the one she wanted." That comment sure made me feel proud, knowing that I was wanted by Grandma and just what she would do to get me. With the afternoon disappearing, I was instructed to pack my belongings. I was going home with Grandpa and Grandma.

# CHAPTER FIFTEEN

# *Time to Heal*

It takes time to heal. It takes time for vivid memories to fade. Time moves at the same pace, by no means faster, in no way slower.

When we got back to Grandma's house it was dark outside. That was okay with me. I knew my way around her house from when I stayed with her the previous summer. I was tired and emotionally drained, so I went upstairs into what would be my bedroom. I did say a little prayer for Mama because I still thought of her often. Then I crawled into bed. I must have been there all of five minutes before I fell asleep.

When I woke up the next morning, I dressed and went downstairs. Grandma greeted me with, "Good morning." I could see she had the table set for breakfast, and even had a bottle of that good tomato juice I helped her and Grandpa preserve in the summer.

Grandpa was sipping his coffee. He told me, "Billy, today we will get you registered in school." The school I would be attending was only four blocks away from their house. There was a convenient neighborhood grocery store right across from the school. That store carried a little bit of everything you might need.

I thought the school was kind of neat; its name was North School. I think it was the oldest school building in Spencer. My classroom was on the second floor, near the fire escape. I thought the fire escape was really different and interesting. It looked like it was a big round metal tube that was fastened to the side of the building. It was sloping downward from the second floor. Some of the boys would jump in it and slide down to the ground. I was afraid to do it because I thought I might get into trouble. I sure didn't want that and have to face Grandma with her heavy-duty utility yardstick she got at the fair. It looked so strong I don't think she could ever break it across my butt, but I wasn't taking any chances.

I liked going to that school. The kids didn't know who I was or where I came from. They only knew I was staying with my grandma, and I liked it that way. I needed some time to get adjusted to all the events that had recently happened to me.

Our teacher's name was Mrs. Jones. I truly liked her, and she was nice. She helped me a lot; she understood my situation and knew there would be times I just wanted to be alone. She knew the emotional load I was carrying, and she understood. Sometimes I stayed after school fifteen or twenty minutes just to talk to her, which would make me feel better. Afterward I would hurry to get to Grandma's house, so she wouldn't get wise to what was going on. I did get some pretty good grades in her class, even though there were times my mind would wander. One time after school I stopped by the store. I had a nickel and was able to buy five penny postcards. The first card I would send would be to Norm Willis, to tell him I lived with my grandma in another town and wouldn't be able to sweep the floors in his grocery store for him anymore.

On Sundays, I went to Sunday school at a little church only six blocks south of Grandma's house. It was kind of fun hearing about how to do good things. It was just like some of the things Mama would talk about, and there I could express some of the values I had been taught. It might seem rather strange, but on Sundays that little bit of talking I did helped me with my emotions. It also helped me to decide to send a thank-you postcard to Bert and one to Fred, and explain why I wasn't around to bug them anymore.

It was cold and snowy outside. I asked Grandpa, "Do you still back your Model T Ford out of the garage and wipe the dust off?"

He said, "I won't shovel the snow from in front of the garage door in the wintertime just so I can back the T out. It will have to wait until spring. Then I will give it a bath and clean it up really good for the summer."

I told him I sure wanted to blow that *ah-ooga* horn again; I liked the way it sounded. That tickled Grandpa. That winter we played cards just about every evening, except the evening we had to listen to the Great Gildersleeve on the radio. That radio program was Grandma's favorite. When she listened to it, there would be times she would slap herself on her knee and laugh so hard, tears would be running down her face. It seemed like she would carry on like she did playing cards. The only difference was she didn't hoot and howl or do her little dance.

Soon it was summertime. The memories of Mama began to start fading, and my internal feelings didn't hurt nearly as bad. The memories weren't as vivid as they used to be; however, her memory would always be permanent with me.

This summer would be different for me. Grandma ruled that I couldn't leave their property without permission. I knew she loved me and wanted to know where I was because she cared. I guess you might say I was in a triple generation gap, and you know that is the worst kind. Let me explain what a triple generation gap is. Grandma was older than Papa, so that is one generation. Papa was in his late fifties, which was old enough to be my grandpa, so that is two generations. Then Papa was my papa, so that is three generations. It is kind of hard living in modern times under olden-day rules.

I did ask Grandma if I could go over to the school playground to play marbles with some of the other boys. She said, "You can go as long as you are back here by supper time." She knew it was good for me to start to join with other kids, as it might help me improve my self-esteem significantly.

I did get a bad case of athlete's foot, so every evening Grandma had me soak my foot in a bucket of warm water with three tablespoons of baking soda mixed in. That was an old-time remedy she said was handed down from generations. Really, I didn't know if it did any good. I think just soaking my foot and keeping it clean was best.

Just so I would have something to do in the summer, Grandma taught me how to crochet. She said, "I will pay you fifty cents for each piece of the lace pattern you make for the pillowcases that are forty inches long."

She would sew the lace on pillowcases to give them a nice frilly edge. I would sit on the couch she had on the front porch and make that crochet hook do its magic. From time to time, I would step on one end of it and stretch it as much as I could. That way, I could get the fifty cents sooner, I thought. In no way was I worried about being embarrassed crocheting in front of the other kids in the neighborhood, because Grandma had scared them off so they never came around to ask me to play with them.

I mowed the lawn for Grandpa. It always took me a lot longer than it should because I would pretend it was Fred and Bessie's lawn, and I had to be careful of all the flowers. I would carefully mow around the flowers, and afterward I would hand-cut the grass I couldn't cut with the mower, just like Fred would do to make the flowers look really pretty. I sure missed going over to Fred and Bessie's. Of course, all during the summer months Grandpa and I helped Grandma can vegetables and make tomato juice, and soon it was the fall season.

The county fair would be starting in another week. It was claimed to be the largest county fair in the world. Grandma said, "You can park cars on our lawn and garden area and charge a dollar for each car. At the end of the day I will split the money with you, and that way you will have some money to buy Christmas presents."

I thought that sounded pretty good, so when the fair started that Saturday, I was right out next to the street yelling at every car that went by. Soon I had the yard and garden area full, a total of sixteen cars. I went into the house, gave the money to Grandma, and she counted out eight dollars for me and eight for her. I took my money and put it in the cigar box in my room.

I went outside again and noticed the vacant lot across the street was empty. I thought parking cars was a pretty good idea, so I went over there and started to park cars.

Soon I had twenty-four cars parked, and I thought I was rich.

About an hour later, Grandpa said, "The person that owns the lot across the street is at the door and wants to see you. His name is Dean Jasper."

I went to the door and there Dean was. He asked me, "Are you the young man who did such a wonderful job of parking my lot full of cars?"

I said, "Yes, I am."

He said, "Now we seem to have a money issue."

I quickly handed him the twenty-four dollars I had collected and said, "Would you like to split it, like Grandma did with me?"

I could see he was thinking. Then he came back with, "I tell you what, I will keep this money, and anyone you park the rest of the day you can have all the money. That way, we won't have to figure out how to split it."

After Dean left the house with all the hard-earned money I had collected parking cars, I told Grandpa what had happened.

That was the first time in my life I heard Grandpa swear, and he even said some words that I heard only once or twice. He was so mad you could almost see steam coming from his ears.

The next day I parked the yard and garden full again for another sixteen dollars. I took it in the house for Grandma to split, and I put my eight dollars in my cigar box. Grandpa wouldn't let me park any cars in the lot across the street, but several people parked there anyway.

Late that afternoon, Dean stopped by the house, only to get a tongue-lashing from Grandpa that he never would forget. Grandpa told him he sure didn't like the way he treated me. It was almost embarrassing how Grandpa talked to him. Grandpa told him by no means would he let me park cars on his lot if I wasn't going to get any money for it. It still didn't make any difference. Dean would not split the money.

During the fair week, we only had half days of school. In the afternoon, I could still park some cars. Grandpa said, "I will take your place in the morning while you are at school, then you can take over when you get home at noon." That sure worked pretty well for me, and Grandma even agreed to the same split.

The fair lasted eight days. By the time it ended, I had earned fifty-six dollars. Now I could plan what I was going to get everyone for Christmas, and Grandpa and Grandma were at the top of my list. I got to thinking that it was sure nice to be able to buy some presents that year, knowing the previous year we had nothing, and what had happened. The vivid memory of losing Mama was now fading, and time was doing a wonderful job of healing.

Considerable time had passed, and soon it was Thanksgiving. Grandma was busy making the noodles a couple of days ahead. She waited until the day before to make the cranberries, and then it was Thanksgiving Day. Grandma was busy with all the cooking, and I was excited because Papa and Mike were coming to dinner, and Uncle Jacob, Aunt Sarah, and Tim would be there, too. Every once in a while I would get to see Tim; he was living with Uncle Jacob and Aunt Sarah. They would come to see Grandma from time to time. I hadn't seen Mike since we left Uncle Jacob and Aunt Sarah's house the past January. I thought, *Wow, that was more than ten months ago.* I wondered if he had changed any, or if he had gotten bigger.

I was almost giddy with excitement knowing I would soon see them. That year, living with Grandpa and Grandma, I would get to eat all the leftovers of some of my favorite foods.

Everyone arrived about thirty minutes before dinner, so that gave us boys a bit of time to talk to each other.

We were all called to the table. We soon found out the talking between us boys didn't stop; in fact, sometimes I caught myself doing more talking than eating. I didn't care because I knew there would be plenty of leftovers the next day, and Mike and Tim would be gone. I was making my time with them count.

When Papa, Mike, and Tim were ready to leave, I went over to Papa and gave him a hug; I did the same with Tim. I gave Mike the biggest hug I had and told him that I missed him. I even had tears running down my face. It was so great to touch him, and that actually made it real for me. When nighttime came, I felt at ease when I went to bed, and, as Grandpa would say, I slept like a log.

A week later I started doing my planning for Christmas. I knew I was going to get Grandpa a polishing kit for his beloved Model T Ford, and I wanted to get Grandma a new whistling teakettle. I wanted to get Papa a fishing lure. On Saturday, I asked Grandma if I could walk down to the Coast to Coast store to buy some Christmas presents.

She said, "It will be all right as long as you aren't away too long." She didn't think I would do it because the store was over two miles from her house.

When I got to the store, a nice lady clerk helped me. I told her what I wanted and asked if she could please wrap them and put them in a sack, so I could carry them home. She said, "The total comes to forty-three dollars and fifty-eight cents." I paid her and started home with my sack of presents. I saved back $12.42. That was in case I didn't get any presents, I could still buy myself one.

When I got back to Grandma's, I was tired from carrying my sack full of presents. First I would carry with one hand, and then the other hand. I had to switch hands often before I got back home. Grandma was surprised when she saw me come in with those presents.

I rested up a little and then set the table for supper, and afterward we were going to play cards.

Soon it was Christmas. Grandma had an artificial tree set up in the living room. All around presents of all shapes and sizes were stacked. I put what I bought for Grandpa, Grandma, and Papa off to the left side of the tree. I didn't know what to expect, because for all of the past Christmases I usually got a gift of clothing and maybe something to play with.

Papa arrived in time to eat. Grandma made a small Christmas dinner of baked chicken, mashed potatoes, gravy, and creamed peas. For dessert we had strawberries that Grandma canned that summer. We were all sitting at the table when Grandma asked, "Billy, would you say grace, please?" I did, and then quietly, to myself, in my own way, I remembered Mama.

I quickly ate. I was excited, and I had never seen so many presents in place at the same time. Papa had brought some presents with him for everybody. After we had cleared the table, Grandpa washed the dishes and I dried them. Then we went to the living room to open gifts. Grandma would hand them out one at a time, wait for that person to open it so everyone could see what he or she got. This was fun. However, I thought to myself, with as many presents as there were, and at the rate we were going, it was going to take all afternoon to open them.

Grandma opened the present I got her, and she was surprised. She even did a little whooping and hollering about her new whistling teakettle. She said, "Just what I wanted. Thanks, Billy."

Grandpa opened the present I got him and said, "What a wonderful present, a polishing kit for my Model T. Thanks, Billy."

Papa opened his and was surprised it was a fishing lure. He said, "Just what I wanted. Thanks, Billy."

I was so happy with all the presents I got: socks, underwear, gloves, a set of checkers, a baseball glove, six new comic books, and some hard Christmas candy. I felt lucky, and the best part was I still had my $12.42 left.

After Papa left, I went up to my room to read some of the new comic books. I was so tired I could hardly hold my eyes open. I started to read and then don't remember what happened until I woke up the next morning.

Sometime after Christmas had passed there was a morning I will never forget. I came down for breakfast and Grandpa said, "I have some bad news for you, Billy. Uncle Jacob was in an accident and was killed last night when a train hit him."

I was stunned. I asked Grandpa to repeat what he had just said. I wanted to make sure I heard it right. Again Grandpa told me about Uncle Jacob.

After Uncle Jacob's services and all the comings and goings of people, we settled back into our normal routine. I would set the table every night for supper, eat, help Grandpa do the dishes, and play cards. That was my routine for most of the winter. Tim continued to stay with Aunt Sarah; she said she didn't want to lose everybody all at once.

When I got my homework completed, the nights we didn't play cards or listen to the radio, I would go to my room to look at the only valuables I had. This was my sock of marbles. I used to look at each one and remember just how and where I got it. After I had carefully reviewed each marble, I would put it in the sock and then put the sock back in my cigar box.

Soon spring was here; the year was 1951. One day when we sat down to eat, Grandma was pouring water into my glass. But she never quit pouring. I shouted, "Grandma, are you okay?" She didn't respond. Then Grandpa told me to go call the doctor because he thought Grandma needed help. I knew how to dial a phone, and Grandma had all the important numbers, for the most part, written on a piece of paper by the phone. I could see Dr. Kingman's number there so I dialed it.

I was in luck. They were working a little late. Beverly, his receptionist, answered the phone, and I told her, "I think my grandma needs help. She is acting strange and she just poured water all over the supper table. Could Dr. Kingman come quickly?"

She said, "Dr. Kingman left a minute ago, but I will try to catch him at the hospital where he went to make his rounds. I will call you back and let you know."

I waited about five minutes, but it seemed like hours before the phone finally rang. I answered it and it was Beverly. She said, "Dr. Kingman is on his way to your house. I told him it was an emergency. He should be there any minute."

The street in front of Grandma's house was graveled. I had just hung up the phone when I saw a car come sliding up to Grandma's house. A man carrying a little black bag jumped out and came running to the front door. When he came in, he said, "I am Dr. Kingman, where is she?"

I said, "Grandpa is taking care of her in the kitchen."

Dr. Kingman rushed to the kitchen and said, "I think she may have had a brain aneurism that burst. She sure is acting like it. We have to get her to the hospital right away." He went to the phone and called for the ambulance to come and get her. Just minutes later the ambulance arrived. Grandma's house was only five blocks from the hospital.

I was concerned because I didn't know what I was going to do if there was no more Grandma. Papa would take Grandpa to see Grandma in the hospital and at night he would stay with us at Grandma's house. I heard him talking to Grandpa about what Dr. Kingman had told him. He was told by Dr. Kingman that Grandma would have trouble talking as well as have trouble with her motor functions if she came through this brain aneurism. I heard Grandpa tell Papa it would be hard at his age to take care of both her and me. I had just heard something I wasn't suppose to hear. I had a lump in my throat. Then Papa said he was going to do what he thought was best for me.

A couple of days had passed when a welfare case worker came to Grandma's house. She was a nice enough lady, but she was all business and never smiled. She showed Grandpa some papers. He read them, and I heard him say he didn't agree at all and wouldn't sign any of them.

About an hour later Papa showed up. He said, "You are to go with the welfare case worker. She will take you to a home for boys and girls because Grandma won't be able to take care of you anymore. Maybe you will get adopted. Get your things packed that you want to take with you."

After I packed what few things I had, Papa put them in the trunk of the welfare worker's car. He signed some papers and told me, "You can ride in the front seat." I knew right then that Papa had abandoned me. He gave me up. I was crushed. The hurt inside was almost unbearable. I looked at Grandpa and could see tears in his eyes. At that moment, I realized Grandpa had been hit with a double whammy: Grandma being in the hospital and losing me to an orphanage. I knew there was nothing he could do.

I was taken to the orphanage without delay.

CHAPTER SIXTEEN

# Orphanage — New Home

I rode in the front seat of the welfare case worker's car all the way from Grandma's house to the orphanage, which was over a hundred miles. I had a lot of time to think about what had happened and plan how I could improve my situation. I didn't know how Grandma was, or when or if she would come home from the hospital. I decided that was something I might never know, and now I must get on with life. I knew I probably would never see her again.

I didn't want to live with a lot of unfamiliar kids. I was ten years old and knew what had happened wouldn't be reversed, since Papa had signed the papers to give me up. I knew I had to make the most important decision of my life. I was as heartbroken as any ten-year-old boy could be. I was devastated. I knew I had to remain positive and determined. Right then and there, I decided I wanted to live my life like Mama had taught me, doing good things. I remembered her telling me you can catch more flies with a spoon of honey than you can with a spoon of lemon juice. I decided I was going to be the spoon of honey. I would be pleasant, smile, and try my best to attract someone to adopt me. I knew that married couples loved kids, and I hoped there was a couple somewhere that would love me.

The welfare case worker said the trip would take about two hours. I entertained myself by holding Kleenex tissue out the window and let it whip in the wind like a flag. I would pretend it was one of the things that made me sad, like seeing Mama so sick. As soon as the wind would shred and rip away the tissue, I would get another and think of another thing that made me sad, like when Uncle Jacob was killed. As soon as the wind would shred and rip it away, I would get another tissue and continue to pretend it was another sad event in my life. I continued doing this until we reached the orphanage. It felt so good to leave my sorrows along the highway, knowing the rain would cleanse me by washing the pieces of tissue away. By the time we got to the orphanage I had used up a whole box of Kleenex.

When we got to the orphanage, we went inside. I waited in the welcoming room while the case worker signed some papers and talked to what I thought was the head administrator. I found I had two penny postcards left, so I decided to send one to Grandma.

I wrote on it, *To Grandma, I hope you get to feel better. I miss you. From Billy.*

Soon, the welfare case worker and the administrator came back in the room and told me from this day forward I could refer to this place as home because this was where I would be living until a family chose me. Then they showed me where I would be staying while at the home. The building had three floors. The top floor was the boys' dormitory. The middle floor was the girls' dormitory, and the first floor was the kitchen, dining hall, and laundry room.

Each floor had a dorm mother, and our dorm mother's name was Mrs. Preacher. She seemed okay, but I could tell that maybe sometimes she could be quite bossy. The boys' dorm had four rows of beds with six beds in a row end to end. My bed was in the third row from the window and fourth bed down the row. Under each bed, there was an open-topped wooden box where we could keep our clothes and any valuables we might have. The boxes were all exactly the same, and you could slide them in and out from under the bed fairly easily.

I only had a couple of bib overalls, three T-shirts, four pairs of socks, some underwear, and my nice brown coat Fred and Bessie gave me for Christmas. I had to leave all my clothes at the laundry. They would mark them so when the lady washed the clothes, she would know whose they were.

The only valuables I had were the marbles I kept in an old sock. I had a couple of big shooters. One was clear all the way through. I never used that one when playing marbles because I didn't want to get it chipped. I had twenty-one of the smaller marbles. I used these a lot when playing with other kids. Those marbles were the most prized possession I had ever had. Lots of times when I was at Grandma's house, I would get them out and try to remember where I had won each one.

Mrs. Preacher told me, "After you put your valuables in your storage box, you can go outside and meet the other kids when they come home from school. Next week you will get to enroll in school, so you can finish the school year and maintain your same grade."

All the kids came home, and the very first ones I met were Tracey and Bob. Both of those boys were a little older than me.

Tracey said, "I have been in the home for five years."

Bob said, "I have been here for three and half years."

Tracey said, "You stick with us, and you won't have to spend much time in the Review."

I asked, "What is the Review?"

Bob spoke right up. "That is where they line us all up for 'orientation,' with prospective parents who want to adopt a child. We are supposed to have our hands and face washed and put on clean clothes, but I never do."

"Me neither," said Tracey. "All the people that come to look for kids don't ever want us older dudes anyway."

Just then, Bob said, "I have to go to the can." So he went in back of one of the trees and relieved himself. He came back and made the remark, "I will do what I want anytime I want to do it. The old lady," he said, meaning Mrs. Preacher, "isn't going to tell me what to do."

The next day I told them I sure didn't like the conversation we had the day before. I told them I didn't like the disrespect they said they displayed at orientation time or some of the slang they were using when referring to people or things.

Tracey said, "Just what makes you so high and mighty? If you aren't careful those prized marbles could come up missing. We know all about your marbles. We don't keep secrets at this place."

I asked, "Will both of you guys wait right here? I will be back as soon as I can."

I went into the home, up to the boys' dorm, and took that sock of marbles out of my storage box. Quickly, I went down the stairs and outside to where Tracey and Bob were. I looked them both in the eye as I held up my sock and asked, "Do you mean these marbles? Is that what you are referring to? I will give them to you now so you won't have to steal them from me. I do stick by what I said about both of you being disrespectful."

Tracey looked surprised, but took the marbles from me, and I went back in the home.

The next day was Sunday. I found a note on my bed. The note said Tracey and Bob were waiting for me out on the edge of the playground by the big oak tree. I thought to myself, *This is only my third day here.* I wondered just what kind of confrontation I had started. I sure didn't want to make trouble. I decided it might be best if I went out there and tried to smooth over the situation. As I walked out to meet them, I thought, *This could be some real trouble.*

After I got there, Tracey was the first to speak. He said, "Bob and I have talked, and both of us agree we were wrong and were being disrespectful. We want to give your marbles back and would like to be friends."

That afternoon, we did have an orientation, and I could see Tracey and Bob had their hands and face washed and had on clean clothes. Even Mrs. Preacher commented on how nice they looked.

At that moment, I knew I had earned their respect, and it would be everlasting, just like Mama said it would be.

A week after school was out, I got to go to outdoor camp. It was located down by the river. I got to sleep in a tent and cook my food over the open fire. The counselors were trying to teach us living skills that someday we might have to use. In the afternoons, I went swimming in the river and totally relaxed, letting my mind

daydream. Before I knew it the week was gone, and I had
to go back to the home.

For the rest of the summer, I got to play with the
other kids in the morning after I got my chores done,
and go swimming in the afternoon at the municipal
pool. Each of us was assigned some chore to do. I didn't
mind drying the dishes after each meal, but I sure didn't
like cleaning the bathrooms. Even though it took a lot
longer to dry the dishes three times a day compared to
cleaning bathrooms once a day, I always volunteered to
dry the dishes.

The last Sunday in June arrived, and that meant orientation again. That afternoon all of us got cleaned up
and put on clean clothes. Traccy and Bob sure looked
nice, and I told them so.

During orientation, I had one lady look at me very
closely. I thought now was the time to be a spoon of
honey, so I grinned and winked at her. She walked a couple of steps past me. After that she came back to me, so I
gave her a second wink. She smiled and again walked a
couple of steps past me. Just that quick, she returned to
look at me once more, so I gave her a third wink. Once
more she smiled and then moved on.

Later in the afternoon, I was outside playing when
Tracey came up to me and said, "Billy, I thought you
were a goner earlier today. I could just tell, by the way

that lady looked at you. Previously, they had picked a girl, so maybe that is why they didn't get you."

I said, "Tracey, we just have to keep trying and maybe one of these times we will get chosen."

Tracey said, "I even notice some of the people were beginning to look at me. I have you to thank for making me realize how to be respectful."

July seemed to go quickly, with my birthday being in the last part. I sure wished I could spend my birthday with Fred and Bessie like I did a couple of years ago. It was fun having cake and listening to her play the piano. It would be a wish come true if they were to come to orientation and pick me. However, at their age I supposed they wouldn't want a young boy around all the time. So my birthday passed without much hoopla. I knew if the home was to give every birthday a big celebration, with as many kids that were there, we would be celebrating all the time.

It was now the last Sunday of the month, and I knew it was orientation time again. Except today, it seemed to feel different for me. I got cleaned up and stood in line like everyone else did. Soon we had three couples come in, and we greeted each of them saying, "Hi," as they walked by. None of them spent much time looking at us. Of course, I smiled and winked at every lady who came through. After about ten minutes it was over, and we were dismissed. I went outside and started playing hide-and-seek.

About an hour had passed when Mrs. Preacher came out and found me. She said, "Billy, you have been chosen, so get in the home and take a bath and put on some clean clothes. Today you are going to a new home."

I was thrilled. I could feel my heart pounding in my chest like no other time before. I was very excited; I even had tears in my eyes. I wanted to find Tracey and Bob to tell them the good news.

Suddenly, I had an idea. I went running to the home as fast as I could, up to my storage box under my bed. I retrieved my most prized passion, my sock of marbles. I took them with me outside and quickly found Tracey and Bob. I gave my marbles to Bob and told him to split them with Tracey. It is my gift to them, so they would have something to remember me by. Then I told them the good news. I had been chosen. I was going to a new family who had a real home. I got to talk to them a little. The man didn't say much but he smiled a lot. The lady was pleasant to talk to; she seemed nice. We talked about going to school, and things to eat, so I thought maybe she would be a good cook, too. They lived on a farm and had some chickens and animals.

Then I said, "You guys keep smiling and winking at the ladies, and you too may be chosen."

Bob told me, "Thanks for the marbles."

Then Tracey spoke up. "We will always remember you, Billy, and how you helped us to be respectful."

I went back into the home, took a bath, and put on clean clothes. I took the time to write Fred, using my last postcard.

I wrote: *To Fred, thank you for letting me come over to your place and thank Bessie for all the good food I ate. I have a new mom and dad now and they live far away from where you live, so I can't come to your place anymore. Good-bye, I will remember you. From Billy.*

As I packed my possessions, I silently bid farewell to all my friends. I knew how lucky I was. I felt energized and excited. I had been chosen. It was time for me to leave my colorful past. I whispered, "Thank you, Mama, for teaching me good values to live by."

Now I was going to begin my new life with my new mom and dad on their farm.

# *Acknowledgments*

Thanks go to my wife of forty-seven-plus years, Connie Peters, who supported and encouraged me to write this book.

I would like to thank my daughter-in-law Julie Speltz Peters for her help with the editing.

And I must thank my friend William Waack for assisting with the front and back covers.

# About the Author

Charles Peters was born near Hartley, Iowa. His childhood was filled with colorful events, some of which he had no control over; they just happened. He spent a short period of time in an orphanage before being adopted by foster parents when he was eleven years old. He grew up in northwest Iowa, graduating from the Lytton Consolidated School. After a career of working first in the dairy industry and then for a major hydraulic manufacturer, he retired in 1998. He currently lives with his wife of forty-seven-plus years in Eden Prairie, Minnesota.

· Living in a scenic area for the past thirty years has enabled him to enjoy nature's beauty and wildlife. In his backyard, he has seen wild animals such as deer, raccoons, fox, and coyotes, and wild birds like turkeys, ducks, geese, and a barn owl. The works of nature can be thrilling and soothing at the same time. He has been influenced by nature's beauty for years.

He felt Billy's story had to be told before it was forgotten forever.

CPSIA information can be obtained at www.ICGtesting.com
Printed in the USA
BVOW042137120313

315396BV00001B/8/P